PRAISE FOR THE SAMANTHA KIDD MYSTERIES:

"...the book is enriched by the author's cleverly phrased prose and convincing characterization. The surprise ending will satisfy and delight many mystery fans. A diverting mystery that offers laughs and chills." *-Kirkus Reviews*

"an impressive cozy mystery from a promising author." *-Mystery Tribune*

"Designer Dirty Laundry shows that even the toughest crime is no match for a sleuth in fishnet stockings who knows her way around the designer department. A delightful debut." -Kris Neri, Lefty Award-Nominated author of *Revenge For Old Times' Sake*

"Combining fashion and fatalities, Diane Vallere pens a winning debut mystery...a sleek and stylish read." -Ellen Byerrum, National Bestselling author of the Crime of Fashion mysteries

"Vallere once again brings her knowledgeable fashion skills to the forefront, along with comedy, mystery, and a saucy romance. *Buyer, Beware* did not disappoint!" *-Chick Lit Plus*

"Fashion is always at the forefront, but never at the cost of excellent writing, humorous dialogue, or a compelling story." -*Kings River Life*

"A captivating new mystery voice, Vallere has stitched together haute couture and murder in a stylish mystery. Dirty Laundry has never been so engrossing!" -Krista Davis, *New York Times* Bestselling Author of The Domestic Diva Mysteries

"Samantha Kidd is an engaging amateur sleuth." -*Mysterious Reviews*

"It keeps you at the edge of your seat. I love the description of clothes in this book...if you love fashion, pick this up!" -*Los Angeles Mamma Blog*

"Diane Vallere takes the reader through this cozy mystery with her signature wit and humor." -Mary Marks, *NY Journal of Books*

"The Samantha Kidd Mysteries continue to be completely fun and entertaining." -*Carstairs Considers*

Ranch Dressing

RANCH DRESSING: A Samantha Kidd Mystery

Book 15 in the Killer Fashion Mystery Series

A Polyester Press Mystery

This is a work of fiction. Characters, places, and events are the product of the author's imagination or are used fictitiously. Any resemblance to real people, companies, institutions, organizations, or incidents is entirely coincidental.

e-ISBN: 9781954579934

Print ISBN: 9781954579965

a killer fashion mystery

Ranch Dressing

DIANE VALLERE

Polyester Press
READING, PA

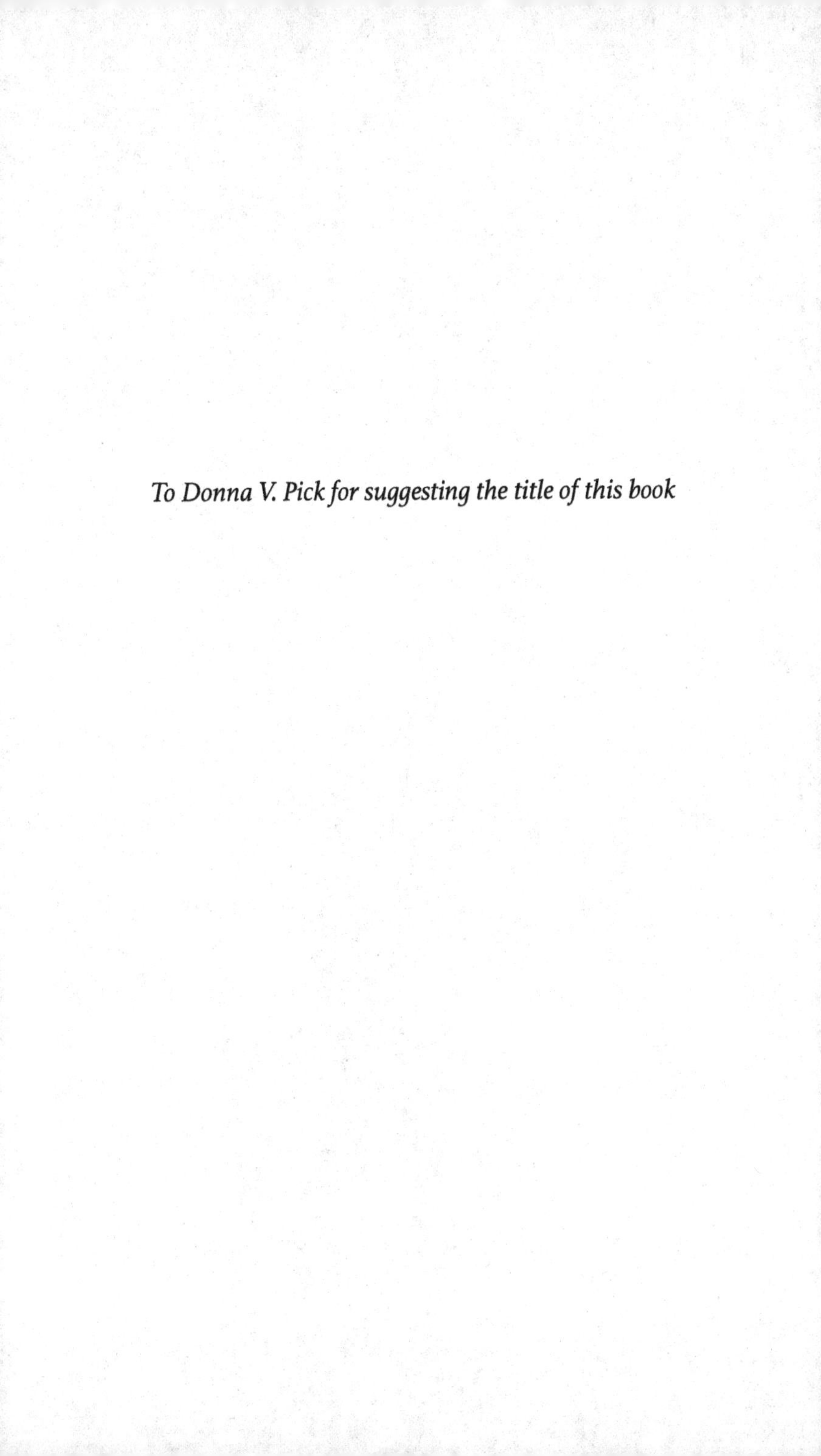

To Donna V. Pick for suggesting the title of this book

1

ASKING TO BORROW CLOTHES

"I need to borrow some clothes," I said. "Jeans," I added then tacked on "Wranglers," for further clarification. I finished with "please" to properly convey my desperation.

As a former fashion buyer with a history of overindulging in wardrobe choices to fit any social setting, I had to be desperate to be standing on the porch of the very unfashionable Detective Loncar, asking to borrow clothes.

Loncar, to his credit, didn't respond right away. We had a complicated relationship, built over years of battling ne'er-do-wells like a modern-day Batman and Robin—my words, not his— in our hometown of Ribbon, Pennsylvania, but at the end of the day, clothes were my wheelhouse, and crime was his. I had stepped over the line too many times to pretend today's request was anything but inevitable.

Loncar was a man of few words, so I wasn't entirely surprised when, instead of replying, he turned around and headed back into his house. I interpreted it as an invitation to join him, so I entered, too, and closed the door behind me. He glanced over his shoulder once, grunted something, and went into his kitchen. By the time I caught up (distracted as I was by the collection of Hummel figurines that I never would have expected to find on display in his living room), he held two mugs of hot, steaming coffee. I almost forgot about the Butterscotch Krimpets that I'd brought with me to soften him up. I raised my hand to indicate the box. (I needed to borrow a week's worth of jeans, so I knew better than to show up with just one package.) He jutted his chin toward his kitchen table, and moments later we were settled in for breakfast.

As long as I had a Butterscotch Krimpet in front of me, I didn't care so much that he had yet to grant my request. I tore open the plastic wrapper and bit into the sweet butterscotch cake. After a few bites, I swallowed. I took a sip of my coffee and almost spit it back out. I set down my mug.

"Decaf," Loncar said.

"Why?"

"Heart."

"Oh. Okay." I picked up my mug and took another sip, this time bracing myself for the tinny taste.

Loncar stood and snatched my mug out of my hand.

He carried both of our mugs to the sink and dumped the contents.

"Hey! I was drinking that!"

"No, you weren't." He opened his fridge and pulled out two bottles of water. Water and Krimpets aren't that solid a combination, but with Loncar's health hanging in the balance, I was willing to make the sacrifice.

"So... do you want to talk about it?" I pointed to his chest, where I presumed his heart would be, though at the moment, he looked a little like a man who had been born without one.

"Ms. Kidd, why are you here?"

The first time I'd met the detective, he had called me Ms. Kidd, not only because it was my name but because I was a suspect in his murder investigation and that was what Emily Post deemed appropriate in such social settings. I'd told him to call me Samantha, but it didn't stick. He'd told me to stop calling him Detective after he retired from the police force, but I didn't listen either. I would always think of him as a homicide detective, which explained my choice of what to call him. His choice to continue treating me like a murder suspect was unsettling, to say the least.

"Like I said, I need to borrow some jeans. Back when we solved that case involving the secret society, I noticed we wear the same size."

Loncar raised both of his eyebrows, which could have been a response to my reference that we'd worked in tandem on an investigation—probably not how he'd describe it even if it was the truth—or that our wildly different body types somehow put us both into 36x30 jeans.

"I thought clothes were your métier?"

"My met… Yes. Right. They were. They are. Yes."

"And I thought you wrote a column for the *Ribbon Times* about how to dress for any occasion?"

"Yes. I do. I did. I'm on a break."

Loncar raised his eyebrows and swallowed a few gulps of water. His Krimpet went untouched.

"Nick's dad is thinking about buying a dude ranch in New Jersey. We're headed there tomorrow, and I don't have anything to wear." The words came out in a rush. "I was going to go to Boot Barn, but then I remembered you, and I thought maybe…" Despite all of the initial gusto I'd used to explain myself, my voice trailed off. "I drove by your office the other day, and there's a For Rent sign in the window. I called, but the number has been discontinued. I tried to reach your daughter, but the calls go directly to voicemail, and when I called Patti, she said you two haven't, um, hooked up for a while."

Patti was the local coroner and was also thirty years Loncar's junior. Neither one of us mentioned that this last fact could have easily been explained by her coming to her senses.

"Patti and I did not have an exclusive arrangement. I'm operating my PI business out of my house while I look for a better location for my office. My daughter went on vacation. She's on a cruise, and she didn't pay for Internet."

"So you're fine? Loncar Investigations is fine? Your heart is fine?"

"Ms. Kidd, your concern is touching." He picked up a Krimpet and bit into the end. I know how tempting a Krimpet can be, and while it surprised me that he'd made it this long without taking a bite, the timing of him doing so seemed more like a display of "everything's fine" than an actual appetite for the most perfect baked good to come out of Philadelphia. He set the rest of the Krimpet on his napkin and stood. "How long will you be gone?"

"A week. We leave tomorrow. Honestly, I'm probably just going to relax by the fire, catch up on my reading, and enjoy the open air. Senior knows as much about running a ranch as I do, and Nick is just indulging his dad." I pushed my plate away from me. There was no way I was finishing mine if Loncar didn't finish his. No. Way. I had as much resistance as the next person, even if that next person was a sixty-something former homicide detective with a possible heart condition. "People make snap judgments based on other people's clothes. I won't look as out of place if I have jeans that are already broken in."

"*People* or you?" Loncar asked. His question did not feel rhetorical.

My resistance wavered, and I took another bite of Krimpet. Loncar was right about fashion being my world, and not long ago, my bursting closet(s) had indicated as much. But I'd hit a wall in my personal growth and, in a fit of radical self-awareness, freed myself from the chains of my past by divesting myself of my past wardrobe choices. These days I lived by a code of simplicity which meant if I borrowed what I needed, my code would remain unbroken.

"It's fine," I said dismissively. "If you don't want to loan them to me, I'll go buy some."

Loncar studied me for a few seconds before responding. This wasn't particularly odd behavior from him. Even though this was an innocent social call, his professional training taught him to keep quiet and let other people fill conversational silence with confessions of guilt.

I didn't like silence. It made me start asking questions. But I'm suspicious by nature, but the only professional training I've had is how to increase gross profit margin on a trending shoe collection.

"Come back later this afternoon. I'll have something ready for you." He stood. I stared up at him. He held his hand out in the direction of the door. I didn't move. "Thanks for the Krimpets."

It was as much a dismissal as a thank-you, but I'd gotten what I came for—or I would. I stood up and went to leave then doubled back, wrapped up the uneaten half of my Krimpet, and carried it out to my car. I'm not ashamed to say I finished it before reaching the traffic light at the end of Loncar's street.

———

LATER THAT AFTERNOON, my father-in-law dropped by unexpectedly for an early dinner. Nick Sr.—Senior to me—was dressed in a shirt made from a blue bandana print, broken-in jeans, and cowboy boots. He carried a pizza from Brothers.

"Change of plans," he said. "We're leaving tonight after dinner."

"I can't leave tonight!" I exclaimed. "I'm not packed."

"It's a week on a ranch," Nick said casually. Like his father, he wore a western-cut shirt, his in a faded print of sage green, ochre, and blue flowers. "Nobody's going to care if you're in a T-shirt and jeans. Didn't you say you planned to sit by the fire and catch up on your reading?"

"Yes, but I made arrangements—"

"Charlie called me," Senior said. "I swung by his place earlier. He gave me a bag. Said you'd know what it was."

"You talked to Detective Loncar? How was he?"

Senior looked at me as if I was asking the wrong question. "He's fine. He said you told him about the ranch." Senior scowled. "Loose lips blow deals like this."

"But Detective Loncar is your wingman," I said. Nick's expression warned that I was on the brink of encouraging something that needed no encouragement. "I didn't think you'd mind me telling him. I'm surprised you didn't invite him to join us."

"Charlie's got his own business problems. I don't need to drag him into mine."

I took the pizza and carried it to the kitchen. "What problems?"

"It's an expression, Kidd. Get me a beer, and let's eat before this goes cold."

———

IT's uncommon for one to go on a road trip and not know what one has packed. Especially when that one is me. I used to work in the fashion industry, and travel was a regular part of my job. I knew how to pack a week's worth of clothes in carry-on luggage. That included options for cocktails and exercise along with daily work attire.

I've always prided myself on dressing appropriately for any occasion, but the last place I ever expected to find myself was a dude ranch in New Jersey. And the last person I ever expected to pack for me was the same detective whose wardrobe I once critiqued while holed up in an interrogation room. My, how I've grown.

Besides, there had to be a clothing shop somewhere near the ranch. No way the ranch would be totally isolated from civilization, right?

2

———

LUMBERJACK EXTRAS IN A
HALLMARK MOVIE

"Welcome to the Down Home Ranch!"

The couple who greeted us looked the part of ranch owners. He wore a plaid shirt tucked into a pair of well-worn Wranglers. The Wranglers were held up by a thick black leather belt with a gold buckle that had been dulled with age. On the man's feet were scuffed cowboy boots. The woman next to him wore a floral peasant shirt over a pair of fitted bell bottoms and red cowboy boots. They both wore cowboy hats. If they hadn't been framed out by an iron gate that said Down Home Ranch, I might have thought they were headed to a costume party.

The two of them walked toward us. The man approached Senior and held out his hand. "I'm Joey Baldwin," he said. "You must be Nick."

"We've got two Nicks in our party," Nick's dad said. "Call me Senior."

"Generous of you," Joey said. They shook hands, then Joey turned to my Nick. "You must be the son."

"Nick Taylor." He shook Joey's hand then turned to me. "This is Sam—"

Joey turned his back on Nick while he was in mid-introduction. "This yours?" he asked, reaching into the back of Nick's truck and grabbing a suitcase.

I stepped forward and reached out for the handles. "That's mine. I'm Samantha."

Joey glanced my way while we both held the handles of Loncar's bag. He kept his hand on the bag and turned to Senior. "Come on inside. I'll send someone out to get the rest of your things." He gave the bag a yank, and it left my grip. He turned away and carried it inside.

"Don't mind Joey," the woman said. "He wasn't expecting you to arrive until tomorrow." She gave me a broad smile. "I'm Kathy."

"Samantha Kidd," I said. "Nice to meet you."

I followed Kathy into the main house. Whatever I'd imagined when Senior told us he was looking at buying a ranch, this wasn't it. The house had thirty-foot ceilings with exposed wooden beams on the interior. The furniture was leather, and the rugs, colorful at one point, had faded into muted shades of red, orange, and turquoise. Photographs of men working with horses hung framed on the walls alongside horns and tackle. A vivid oil painting of a cowboy rounding up cattle hung above the mantel. I paused for a moment while I was taken by the energy of it: the horse's muscles in motion, the man in the saddle, the cattle in the foreground, all captured in shades of beige, camel, rust, and brown, with a blue sky setting it off. A skull bleached to white by the sun hung on the wall to the left of the painting. The closest I'd ever been to an interior like this was the last time I ate at the LongHorn Steakhouse.

"You've never been to a ranch before, have you?" Kathy asked.

"Is it that obvious?"

She stepped back and scanned my outfit. I'd been so thrown by the idea of leaving early that I'd spent my post-pizza time on my overnight kit and hadn't taken the time to change out of my ivory funnel-neck sweater and corduroys. Surrounded as I was by the colors of dirt, mud, and sky, I felt conspicuous in a way I rarely had.

"I didn't expect us to arrive today either," I joked.

A fire blazed on the right-hand side of the interior. From a room beyond the entrance, pots clanged and voices shouted. The scent of steak wafted through the interior, mingled with other savory smells like sweet corn, butter, and freshly baked bread.

"Chef already served dinner, but he's preparing something for your party." Kathy turned away from me and called to two men dressed like lumberjack extras in a Hallmark movie. The older one had gray hair and a beard streaked with white. He was thin and wiry. The younger one, about thirty years his junior, had black hair and sideburns styled like Elvis in his later years. "Cody, Angus, the Taylor party is here. Bring the rest of their luggage in from the truck out front and put it in their rooms."

The two cowboys nodded and went outside. The younger cowboy made eye contact and tipped his hat at me. "Howdy, ma'am," he said. "Welcome to the Down Home Ranch."

"Hi." I pressed my lips together and stifled a giggle, feeling my face grow warm. I averted my eyes, and the cowboy hoisted two bags and carried them into the hallway. I caught Kathy watching me.

"Best steer clear of Cody," she said. "He's a massive flirt, and unless he gets the signal you're not interested, that wedding ring on your finger isn't going to do much to deter him."

"I should go find my husband."

"That's a good idea," she said. "He's probably out back with Joey." I turned to leave, and she put her hand on my arm to stop me. "This isn't like the real world, Samantha. We all have roles: the men run the place, and the women are here to support them."

"You don't actually believe that, do you?"

"I believe your father-in-law is thinking about buying the ranch, and I believe he'll have a much easier time making his decision if he understands what people expect of him. Assuming you want what's best for him, you'll put aside your preconceived notions about our power dynamic and act accordingly."

"When you put it like that..." I stepped back and

looked up at the ceiling then around at the walls. "How long have you and Joey owned the ranch?"

"It's been in his family for three generations. Joey always expected to pass it down to our children, but we didn't have any. About twenty years ago, we converted it from a working cattle ranch to a cowboy experience for the public. We employ ranch hands to manage the horses, and we make most of our income booking parties and private events."

"Senior is in his seventies. He's older than your husband. I don't know how much hands-on experience he's going to want to give."

"I assumed you and your husband were going to come with him to manage the day-to-day running of the place," she said, "until I saw your outfit."

I felt my face flush again, this time in embarrassment. In the past, I'd thrived when my unique style set me apart from the crowd, but that had always been a conscious choice. Fashion had been my armor. But today, my fashion faux pas was bringing me a different level of attention, and I didn't like it.

I glanced at the bags that had been stacked behind the leather sofa for the one Loncar had packed for me. It wasn't there.

"Is something wrong?" Kathy asked.

"One of my bags is missing." I looked toward the front door. "The one Joey carried in."

"He probably took it to your room."

"I don't think so," I protested.

"We'll get it sorted in the morning."

I was about to protest again, to tell her that I needed the bag—overnight necessities and whatnot—but before the words were out of my mouth, an orange-and-white blur ran past me and darted out the front door.

"What was that?" I asked.

Kathy scowled. "That was one of the barn cats. They get in here when someone leaves the door open. He must have snuck in while the men were bringing in your luggage."

"Speaking of luggage," I said, "I do need my bag tonight. Pajamas," I added, even though I was pretty sure Loncar hadn't thought to include them.

"I'll have someone bring you something to sleep in and an overnight kit, and we'll get your bags sorted out in the morning." She smiled at me, but something in her expression didn't read as friendly. I'd been at the Down Home Ranch for less than fifteen minutes, and already I felt like I was an inconvenience.

Nick and Senior came back inside. Wherever they'd been, it had brought out the ruddiness in their complexions and excitement in their eyes. About thirty years were between them, but the similarities were more obvious now than ever.

"Whoo!" Senior clapped his hands together and rubbed them as if to warm them up. "That was some ride."

"Ride?"

"Joey took us out to the stables. He had a couple

horses suited up. We took them out to patrol the perimeter of the ranch. It's something out there."

"You've already been out on horses? You already saw the rest of the ranch?"

Nick studied me. "You're not jealous, are you? I thought you were going to spend your time here reading Louis L'Amour."

"I just didn't expect you to start your great western adventure tonight. You said Joey had the horses already saddled up and ready to go? How did he know we were coming tonight? Kathy acted like they still expected us tomorrow like we originally planned."

But Nick didn't answer me, or if he did, I didn't hear him. Instead, I heard the screech of brakes right before the shriek of metal silenced it.

3

NO JUDGMENT HERE

I forgot all about my missing bag and ran to the entrance. The door was solid wood, ten feet high, and reinforced with cross beams, and it took a bit of muscle for me to pull it open. When I did, I saw a small white car wrapped around a telephone pole. A man and woman were inside the car. The passenger-side door opened first. I ran to the car, and my heel slipped through the muddy ground. I lost my balance and fell forward, my hands landing on the exterior of the bent vehicle. Mud kicked up around the bottom of my ivory corduroy jeans. I yanked the car door open and helped the man inside unhook his seat belt then held my hands out to him while he reached for balance. Nick was at the driver's side, helping a woman exit the vehicle at the same time. We guided the couple to a bench outside the ranch, where they sat next to each other.

"I'll wait with them," I said to Nick. "Go inside and get help."

"On it," Nick said. He left.

I was already too dirty to care about the state of my clothes, so I knelt down in the muddy ground in front of the couple. It felt cool through the knees of my corduroys. The man and woman appeared to be fine, if shaken, but I still tried to remember what to do in a case of possible concussion.

"State your names," I said.

The man looked at me. "We're not trespassers. We're paying guests. Is this how you welcome people?"

"Calm down, Billy," the woman said, putting her hand on his arm. "It's not her fault her cat charged in front of the car."

"No, it's your fault for slamming on the brakes and losing control of the car. I knew I should have driven."

"You couldn't drive. You had three drinks at dinner."

"I never wrapped the car around a phone pole."

I couldn't tell from their banter if this was how they always communicated or if this was the result of the trauma experienced by their accident. Neither had stated their names like I'd requested, but they both appeared to have their wits about them—wit enough to lay blame on each other.

Like everyone else I'd met so far, they were each dressed in standard-issue western wear. I recognized the woman's shirt and jeans from the Wrangler website. Her denim jacket had a Sherpa collar and cuffs, and she'd forgotten to snip the tag from where it dangled under her arm.

The man's clothes looked equally new. He wore a black shirt with white piping, embroidered with red roses. His shirt was tucked into dark denim jeans that were being held up by a tooled black-leather belt with a shiny gold buckle. On his feet were pointy black boots embroidered with red flowers that coordinated with his shirt. It was as if they'd saved up their whole life for a week on a ranch and had blown a third of their budget on their wardrobe.

No judgment here. I might have done the same thing if I didn't have an in with Loncar.

"I'm Samantha Kidd," I offered, mainly to interrupt their argument. "I'm a guest too. We just arrived."

The man studied me. "Was that your husband?"

"Yes." I waited for him to say something else, but he didn't.

The woman next to him said, "I'm Lulu Cassidy. This is Billy. We're probably going to be seeing a lot of each other over the next few days."

Billy shook his head at his wife's gregarious behavior. "I hope you ride a horse better than you drive a car."

The door to the ranch opened, and Joey came out. I waited for Nick to follow, but he didn't. Joey squinted through the darkness, stared at the smashed-up car, and turned to us.

"You okay?" he asked.

Billy stood. "We're fine, no thanks to my wife's driving."

"That was your first mistake." Joey tucked a gold horseshoe nail into his shirt pocket and held his hand out for a handshake. "Glad you could make it. Sorry you missed the dusk patrol. We just got back."

Joey put his hand on Billy's shoulder and guided him into the house. I stared at them, equal parts curious about and disgusted by Joey's behavior. He'd barely acknowledged Lulu, except to insult her, and left her sitting alone on the porch after a somewhat-traumatic experience. It seemed I wasn't the only one bothered by the unfolding events because the orange-and-white cat strode across the dirt track in front of the ranch and brushed up against Lulu's ankles. She glanced down at him, as if deciding whether or not to blame him for the accident, then reached down and scratched his ears.

"I never could resist a cat," she said. "Especially when they run in front of the car."

"I would have done the exact same thing," I said conspiratorially then added, "except for the telephone pole part." Lulu looked at me nervously, as if expecting another insult. "I probably would have cut the wheel to the right and crashed into the barn."

My display of solidarity was met with a smile.

The cat jumped up on the swing and nestled in between us. It was dark, and a hint of color—lively orange by the horizon—remained to the night sky. Above us, a blanket of stars was set against a deep, bottomless purple-blue background. The light came from the moon, a glowing orb not quite full but close. A breeze swept over us, and I reached up and held my hair away from my face and closed my eyes. I could hear the chirp of crickets, the call of owls, and the mix of male voices coming from inside the house. It was peaceful in a way I wasn't used to, and it had the effect of a cold glass of water on a hot day—something pure and simple to nourish the body and mind.

My stomach growled, interrupting the peaceful night sounds. The cat lifted his head and stared at me. I ran my hand over his head. I'd forgotten all about the late meal the chef was preparing for us, but now all I could think about was eating.

"Before you arrived, Kathy said the chef was making us a late dinner," I said. "Do you want to head in and eat?"

"Sounds good."

We stood. Lulu picked up the cat and set him on the ground. He followed us into the house, and I didn't do a darn thing to dissuade him. Maybe he was a barn cat who wasn't supposed to be in the main house, but so far, the cat was my favorite part of this ranch experience.

Unlike when my party of three had arrived, the main portion of the house was empty. The fire still roared in the fireplace, casting off light and warmth, but the leather seats were all vacant. I hadn't gotten the tour, but I remembered Kathy gesturing to the rear left when she mentioned the chef, so I led Lulu that way. I pushed through a set of saloon-style doors and found Joey seated at a large wooden table with Senior, Nick, and Billy. Joey leaned back. He had a long gold nail between his fingers, and he tapped it on the tabletop. Nick's expression was troubled. He glanced down at my sweater and motioned toward his chest.

"What happened to you?" Senior asked.

"I was out front with Lulu." I didn't mention that she'd just been in a car accident because at least three of the people seated at the table already knew that. Besides, I was distracted by the empty plates in front of those three people. Nick's plate held what appeared to be a full portion: beans, rice, corn on the cob, and a biscuit. Bowls in the center of the table had been picked over.

"You look like you got the wrong end of a bronco," Senior said. He looked at Joey, who laughed along with him.

I glanced down at my sweater. From the moment I had heard the crash out front, I'd forgotten all about my wardrobe crisis, but I was back to being the center of attention. From the knees down I was splattered with mud like a Jackson Pollock panting, and my ivory sweater had clumps of dried dirt and matted orange cat hair. My hands were filthy, too, and I could imagine what my face and hair looked like. I turned back to Lulu, who was pristine in her chambray shirt and faded jeans. It wouldn't have killed her to say something while we were bonding.

"You'll want to clean up before you eat," Joey said, not

making eye contact. "We don't bring the outdoors to the dinner table. We've got rules about that."

"It would have been nice if someone told us dinner was ready," I retorted.

"The food'll keep while you change," Joey said. "Might get cold, but there's a price to pay for tardiness."

I glared at the ranch owner, this time engaging muscle groups I rarely used to keep myself from responding. While I felt steam build up behind my ears, he just sat there, watching me while idly playing with his gold spike. I was here as Senior's guest. If all went as planned, Senior was either going to buy the ranch from Joey or chalk the week up to a new experience. Either way, I'd never have to see this man again.

A week. Maybe two. I could last that long. I had the complete works of Zane Grey and a barn cat at my disposal. Nobody said I had to socialize.

"Where's our room?" I asked Nick.

He stood. "We're down the hall. Last door on the right."

"I'll be right back."

Even though I was almost ready to pass out from hunger (I'm not known for going long between meals, and by meals, I mean snacks too), I held my head high and left the dining room. *Don't let him get to you. Don't let him get to you. Don't let him get to you.* I chanted the words with each step, so focused on my own misery that I didn't realize someone was inside my room.

It was Cody, the flirtatious cowboy. Was this ranch just one landmine after another?

"Hi," I said, startled to find him there.

"Howdy." He glanced at my sweater. "Reckon you came in here to change before dinner."

"You reckon right."

Cody raised his eyebrows. His face was tan, and the creases by his eyes were deep. His eyes were bright blue, like those of every person who had ever been cast in a Western, and I know that because I watched five of them to prep for this trip. (Six if you counted *City Slickers*, which Senior informed me I could not.)

"Is it *always* like this?" I asked. "Men on the left, women on the right? Like a square dance?"

He chuckled. "You're getting the full ranch experience. Don't put too much stock in what you saw today. Angus and I are cowboys, but Joey and Kathy are about as hands-on as a couple of managers at the local steakhouse. People come to stay at a dude ranch, they want to feel like they're getting an experience they never had. Think of this place like dinner theater. Not a lot here is what it seems."

4

ALONG FOR THE RIDE

I MIGHT NOT BE FAMILIAR WITH THE WAYS OF THE RANCH, but I was more than familiar around things not being what they seemed.

"So this is all an act?" I asked.

"Maybe not all of it, but most," Cody said. "Things are always a little out of whack when guests arrive. Joey likes to set the stage right away. He'll settle into his role tomorrow. And don't count Kathy out just yet. She's a force to be reckoned with too."

He pointed to Loncar's bag, which sat at the end of a row of our luggage. "Found that in the lobby. Must have gotten missed earlier."

"Thank you, Cody."

"Welcome, ma'am." He tipped his hat. "I'll be seein' you in the morning."

My face flushed like it had earlier. I waited until the door was closed behind him and turned the lock for good measure. I unzipped my bag of books and pulled out a T-shirt that said BEEN DOING COWBOY STUFF ALL DAY, a gift from my best friend, Eddie, who was back in Ribbon, cat- and dog-sitting for me and Senior respectively. He was much more likely to feel at home on the range, but this was a family affair, and wrangling an invite didn't seem appropriate. I did promise to bring him back a keepsake. Maybe I'd ask Kathy where she got the painting over the mantel.

I changed into the T-shirt and a pair of Loncar's jeans and went back to the dining room. Nick remained at the table. My brief conversation with Cody had alleviated some of my concerns about the week, so I didn't launch into an attack on our hosts. I sat while Nick slid a plate of food in front of me. I shoveled a forkful of rice and beans into my mouth before speaking. The food was cold, but I didn't care.

After a few bites, I asked, "So what do you think?"

"What I think doesn't matter. My dad loves the place. He's had stars in his eyes from the moment we arrived."

"How was the ride?"

"It's a shame you missed it. The sun was just hitting the horizon, and the light crested over the mountains. It was purple blended into orange. I've never seen anything like it. The only thing I would have changed was to have you with me to share the moment."

Nick and I had been married for a few years, and the bumps we'd hit along the way were due to my instincts to try solving his problems before he asked. I was an innate problem solver, and Nick's shoe design business had taken a dent shortly after he'd proposed. That threw the power balance between us out of whack, and I'd been doing what I could to restore it ever since. This trip, for his father, with me loaded down with nothing but a backpack of books, was my way of saying I didn't have to be involved in everything. Sometimes I could just go along for the ride.

That being said, it was nice to know Nick had missed my company.

"I wish I could have seen it," I said. "Maybe I can come with you tomorrow."

"I'll tell Joey."

Nick kept me company while I polished off the cold rice, the cold beans, the cold corn, and the cold biscuits. By the time I set down my fork, my muffin top took the pole position in my list of problems. I reached down and unbuttoned the top button of Loncar's jeans, getting a teensy bit of relief.

I set my napkin on the table, and Nick stood. I glanced at the mess of empty plates, serving dishes, soiled napkins, and tumblers. "Who cleans up?"

The saloon-style doors by the kitchen swung open, and a man in a white chef's smock came out. "That'll be me," he said.

"Are you the chef?"

"Yup. Call me Chef."

I glanced behind him. "Isn't everybody in the kitchen called Chef?"

"Nope. Nobody else back there." He picked up two empty bowls.

Nick glanced at his watch. "I'm going to go take a shower and wind down. You coming with me?"

"I'll be along in a moment."

It seemed rude not to help clear the table, so I picked up the empty biscuit bowl and my empty glass. I followed Chef into the kitchen and set the dishes on the island next to the ones he placed there.

"You don't have to clear the table here like you do at home."

"To be fair, clearing the table at home is moving the pizza box to the trash."

"You won't find any pizza around here. It's beans and rice, steaks and biscuits. I'll fix you a salad if you request it, but nobody ever requests it. People want to feel like they're on a ranch, so I make ranch food."

"Do you have any pretzels?" I asked. Chef looked at me funny. "Never mind," I muttered.

Despite Chef's protests, I helped clear the table. It felt good to be useful, and it gave me a chance to see a part of the ranch that I might not otherwise. Chef was chatty, pointing out the bins of rice and beans, which did confirm his statement that these were staples of the ranch, along with an entire closet filled with wagon wheel pasta and Slim Jims for the Li'l Pardner menu.

"I appreciate the help, ma'am, but if Joey sees you helping me, I might be out of a job."

"I doubt that. He seems to like it when women do women's work."

"Have to correct you there. Every employee here has a job to do. I'm responsible for the meals, and that means sourcing, making, cleaning. Angus and Cody are the ranch hands. They oversee the horses and patrol the grounds and do just about anything else that comes up during the day. Joey is the ranch owner, and that means making sure the rest of us do what's expected of us."

"What about Kathy? She's a co-owner. Shouldn't she have some responsibility?"

"Don't worry about Kathy," Chef said. "She keeps herself busy."

I wanted to ask how she kept herself busy, what exactly it was that she did, but I sensed the conversation was over. Chef turned the sink water on to full blast, drowning out any more conversation. I stood behind him while he mixed up a basin of hot water, waiting for him to turn it off and chat some more, but he didn't. He pulled out a rag and wiped down all the surfaces while the water level rose. Steam built up in a cloud by the sink, and his arms turned red from plunging into the hot water. At one point, he glanced over at me, seemingly surprised to find I was still there. "Thanks for the help," he said. "Your secret is safe with me."

I managed a smile and waved goodbye.

It was a little after nine p.m. I found Nick asleep in our room. His hair was still damp from his shower. I'd slept for most of the drive here, and between my two-hour nap and my belly full of food, I was too awake to sleep. I unzipped my backpack, pulled out a Zane Grey novel, switched off the lights, and went out front to read by the fire.

There was something unique about the ranch. Earlier today, when we first arrived, it had been bustling with energy—cowboys and horses, down-home cooking, and new arrivals. But it wasn't even ten o'clock, and the place was quiet. I'd counted eight people already and figured they must all be sleeping under this roof, but the silence was pierced by the sounds of the crackling fire. The orange-and-white cat was curled up on a club chair. He raised his head and opened one eye then, appearing to accept that I was not there to disrupt his sleep, laid his head back down on his paws and fell back asleep.

A Tiffany lamp sat on a wooden end table, casting light over the end of the long leather sofa by the fire. I moved a pillow to the end of the sofa then lay down and cracked my book. I was three chapters in when the cat jumped down from his chair and approached the front door. He let out a meow that made it clear what he wanted. He turned and looked at me and meowed again.

Well, that was just great.

I tucked the cover flap into my page and set my closed book on the floor then got up and went to the front door. I grabbed the handle and leaned back, this time letting my weight do the work of opening the door. The cat ran outside into the cool night air and trotted toward the stables.

Something about the scene wasn't right, but I couldn't make much out in the darkness. I stood out front and closed my eyes, allowing them to adjust to the night, then opened them again and scanned the property. The mud out front had dried, leaving the ground rough and uneven, thanks to the skid marks left behind from the accident. The mangled vehicle had been moved away from the telephone pole and had probably been towed to a mechanic or junkyard, depending on the damage.

I turned to the left and to the right, trying to figure out what was bothering me. Movement by the stables caught my eye, and I stood as still as I could, trying to determine what had caused it. A dim light came from inside the stables and illuminated a dirty window. A bulky shape temporarily blocked out the light—then another, then three—before I realized the shapes were horses.

I didn't know anything about life on a farm, but six seasons of *Yellowstone* left me knowing one thing: horses shouldn't be wandering around outside the stables at night while the rest of the ranch slept.

I didn't have the knowledge or the wherewithal to corral the horses on my own, and I knew it. I also didn't know where to find Joey, Kathy, or anybody except for Nick and his dad. I pushed aside my concerns about how the horses had gotten out in the first place and ran back inside, stumbling through the living room with the light from the fireplace to illuminate my path. When I reached my room, I switched on the overhead lights and shook Nick's leg.

"Nick, wake up. Something's wrong. The horses got out of the stable."

To his credit, he woke quickly. In seconds, he was out of bed and dressed. "I'll find Joey. Go outside and try to keep them calm."

We went in two different directions. I didn't know jack about keeping horses calm, but this wasn't the time for ignorance. I cut through the kitchen. A bunch of carrots sat on a cutting board next to a chef's knife. I grabbed the carrots and went out the back door then spoke softly to the first horse I encountered.

"It's okay. I don't know who let you out, but you're fine." I didn't think the horses could understand me, but I didn't know what else to say. "Maybe you can tell me who let you out? I'll give you a carrot if you do."

"What do you think you're doing?" asked a harsh voice.

I turned and recognized Cody, the flirtatious cowboy. He grabbed the carrots from my hand. "You shouldn't be out here." There was nothing flirtatious about his tone.

"The horses got out. The rest of them are in front of the stables."

Cody's body language changed immediately. "Where?"

I pointed. Nick and his dad came around the side of the building. Cody ran toward them and shouted instructions. I watched with interest as they approached the frightened horses and tried to calm them. I was about as helpful as the cat who sat on a tree stump, cleaning his front paw.

"What happened out here?" I asked the cat. Like the horses, he kept his intel to himself.

The lack of light outside the ranch made the task of rounding up the horses more difficult. I went inside the stables to find the light source that had caught my attention in the first place. It was a gas lantern, sitting on top of a bale of hay. The wick was burning down, and the light dimmed. The negligence of abandoning a gas lantern in a stable filled with hay and horses was off the charts, and whether it was an accident or not, I'd have to tell Joey about it tomorrow. I picked up the handle and swung the lantern around the interior of the stables, only to realize how quickly I'd have to change my plans.

The body of Joey lay motionless inside the stable to my right.

5

———

HELPLESS FEMALE

I DIDN'T KNOW A THING ABOUT CORRALLING HORSES, BUT sad to say, I knew what to do about finding a body. I set the lantern on the ground next to Joey and checked his wrist for a pulse. There was none. I glanced around his body to see if anything stood out, like a large, heavy object that might have been used to knock him out. The only thing nearby was the lantern.

The lantern.

The lantern.

It was too late to worry about fingerprints on what very well might have been a murder weapon, and it was too dangerous to leave it behind for the police, so I picked it up again and held it by Joey's head. Sure enough, there was a dark, wet substance matted in his hair. I recoiled and darn near dropped the lantern on the hay. I scrambled backward then pulled myself up and backed out of the stables, bumping right into Cody.

"Go back to the house," he commanded. "This is no place for a helpless female."

I held the lantern out of his reach. "But Joey—"

"Joey would agree."

I stepped away to give Cody an unobstructed path to the stables. "Joey can't agree. He's dead."

The look on Cody's face was nothing short of murderous, which put him at the top of my list of suspicious people. A numbness radiated outward from the center of my chest to my arms and legs, and the horror of the situation dawned on me. I pointed into the stable. "His body is in the last stall on the right."

"Call the police," he said. Before I could stop him, he grabbed the lantern out of my hand and turned away, using the minimal light as a beacon for Nick and Senior as they led two additional horses back to the stables.

I didn't stop to argue, ask questions, or assert my independence. I returned to the house and went straight to the kitchen. A phone was mounted to the wall. I made the call to 911, gave my name and location, and told the operator the nature of my emergency. I stayed on the line while she dispatched the local sheriff, then I wrapped a blanket around my shoulders and went outside to wait for them to arrive.

It didn't take an expert to know this was bad. We were here to determine if the Down Home Ranch was a worthy investment for Nick's dad, and that included getting to know the day-to-day activities of the ranch and getting to meet the existing staff that kept the place running. We'd been here for a total of three hours, and the owner appeared to have been murdered. Of everyone we'd met in our short time, he'd been the least friendly, the least welcoming, and my least favorite of the bunch, but that didn't mean he deserved to die.

But he was dead, and someone had killed him. We were an isolated group of people, and the likelihood was that one of us was the killer. My mind started a quick catalog of people I'd met since first arriving—Kathy, Joey's wife; Angus and Cody, the cowboys; Chef, the, um, chef; Billy and Lulu, the other paying guests. Was that it? Were there only six people who could have done this? Or were there others, such as staff and guests who'd eaten earlier and retired to their rooms or hadn't made their presence known? If a staff member planned to commit a murder, they'd probably keep their distance until the deed was done.

Not long ago, Nick and his business partner were nominated for Sneaker Designer of the Year. The award ceremony had taken place at a hotel in our hometown of Ribbon, Pennsylvania, as had the murder of the toastmaster. A snowstorm had trapped two hundred attendees inside the hotel with the murderer, and as much as I'd tried to keep the lines of communication with the police open, Mother Nature had interfered with that, too, downing phone lines. I learned an important thing about myself during that situation. I didn't like being trapped with a murderer.

But that was a hotel, a self-contained building whose

entrances had been blocked by three feet of snow. This was a twenty-five-hundred-acre ranch, with trails and trees and nature as far as the eye could see. People couldn't come and go easily from a snowed-in hotel, as a few of them found out, but here? This was a criminal's wet dream. Whoever killed Joey in the stables could be seated at a slot machine in Atlantic City by now.

By the time the sheriff arrived, Nick, Senior, and I had moved inside. I found a stash of blankets in a cedar chest and doled them out, and we sat by the fire, waiting to give our statements. Angus and Cody were still outside with the horses while the sheriff conducted a walkthrough of the stables. I volunteered to go with them, to provide a play-by-play of my discovery of the body, but they told me to wait inside. It had been a night of being told what to do, but this time I listened without resistance.

The one thing none of us mentioned was Kathy, Joey's wife. She had been, presumably, asleep somewhere inside the house while an investigation into her husband's murder commenced. The problem was that she was as much of a suspect as the rest of us. It wasn't my place to go knocking on doors like the town crier, not if her response to the news of her husband's murder told the police something about her possible involvement.

I hadn't been tired at quarter after nine, but by two thirty, I was exhausted. The sheriff, an older man with a full head of white hair and matching goatee, came into the house and approached our party of three. He held a green thermos that looked to be from around the time the Boy Scouts were first organized. "Mrs. Taylor?" he asked me. "I'm Sheriff Parker. I'd like to ask you a few questions."

"It's Kidd," I said then clarified, "My last name. I'm Samantha Kidd."

"I thought you were Mr. Taylor's wife."

"I am. I kept my name when we married."

He sat in the club chair across from me and set his thermos on the table between us. I waited for him to unscrew it, to pour himself a cup of coffee into the lid, to make an "I'm a friendly guy" comment about his wife sending him off for the night shift with a thermos of coffee, God bless her, or some other charming banter, but he didn't. He just let the thermos sit there like he was performing a role and the prop department had supplied it to him at the last minute.

He studied me but didn't comment on my name. He may have been waiting for me to fill the silence— perhaps with a proclamation of guilt—like Detective Loncar had done in our early days, but this sheriff didn't know I'd long ago learned that lesson. I kept quiet, too, and the silence blossomed into a peaceful standoff.

"Walk me through your night," Parker finally said, ending our stalemate.

"After I finished helping Chef clean up my late dinner, I went to my room. It was a little after nine. Nick was already asleep, so I got a book and came out here to read."

The sheriff's eyes narrowed, but he didn't ask any questions. He nodded.

"I read about three chapters before the cat meowed to go outside," I continued. "I let him out and saw that the horses had gotten out. I don't know where anybody's rooms are other than my own, so I woke up Nick, and he got his dad. We went out to try to corral the horses back to the stables, and I ran into Cody."

"Seems like you missed a few steps," Sheriff Parker said. "Cody said you had carrots in your hand. Where did you get them? Why did you go into the stables if you were trying to corral the horses? How did you see Joey's body in the dark stables? How did you know he was dead?"

That was a lot of questions in a short amount of time, though none of them were entirely unexpected. "I have some experience with this sort of thing," I said, trying to establish a connection. "This isn't my first rodeo."

"This isn't a rodeo. It's a ranch. And right now, your statement raises more questions about your behavior than answers, so let's keep going."

"That's not what I meant." I chewed my lip and considered telling him about the help I'd given Detective Loncar back home, about the number of homicide cases I'd all but broken wide open. The mayor of Ribbon was due to give me a key to the city any day now.

I kept all of that to myself.

But keep going we did. I gave Sheriff Parker a play-by-play of my time, from letting the cat out, to spotting the loose horses, to waking Nick, to cutting through the kitchen. I told him about the carrots and the cutting board and the lit lantern that I found inside the stables mere feet from Joey's body. I did not share the conclusions I'd drawn about a whole lot of these things because I could not yet tell if Sheriff Parker was a friendly. By the time Parker decided we were done, I had a fresh set of questions too.

I also had a solid reason for not doing anything about my questions—my pact with Nick.

Until tonight, the idea of lying on a sofa under a blanket in front of a cozy fire while reading my way through a stack of books sounded like the getaway I needed. Life had a way of throwing me curveballs, and I'd secretly been looking forward to time on the ranch, even if it meant wearing cowboy boots. I could handle cowboy boots.

It's not like anybody here knew me or the stance I'd taken against western attire back when I was a buyer for Bentley's in New York. That felt like a lifetime ago— before I moved back to Pennsylvania, before Nick and I shifted our relationship from professional to personal, before his father moved in, before I became more known for my crime solving than my fashion sense. I was a completely different person these days. And after my last physical, my doctor suggested if I didn't find a way to relax (that had nothing to do with murderers), the odds were in favor of Nick becoming a widower before his forty-fifth birthday.

But even with my best intentions, I couldn't *not* notice

the suspicious behavior in front of me. We'd been invited to the ranch to stay for a week while Senior considered whether he was up to the task of running it—or, more likely, employing the existing staff to do so under his bankroll. Since our arrival, we'd met both Joey and Kathy, their two ranch hands, and the chef, but there's no way a twenty-six-hundred-acre ranch was run by a mere five people. Sheriff Parker might find the presence of Nick, his father, and me to be suspicious but only because we were visitors and the sheriff had no history with us. But we weren't the only visiting strangers. Billy and Lulu were guests too. If I intended to steer clear of this investigation, maybe my best bet was to make a couple new best friends.

6

THE BARREL RACER

I woke to the steady sound of rhythmic thumping. Light crested in through the faded curtain, spilling over the faded patchwork quilt and Nick's empty side of the bed. I reached out for the clock on the nightstand and turned it toward me. It was nine thirty. Somehow, despite what had transpired last night, I'd managed to sleep in.

Our luggage was lined up along the wall. There was a fifty percent chance that we would be leaving today, assuming the sheriff would allow it, so there seemed no point unpacking until we knew which end was up. I located Loncar's bag and unzipped it to see my options. On top of a pile of jeans was a clear plastic bag packed full of old bandanas.

I pushed the bandana bag aside and pulled out a pair of jeans. They were Wranglers, broken in from decades of wear. Before Loncar's divorce, he'd been shaped like a barrel. I slipped on his jeans, relieved to find that they fit over my hips, and belted the waist. I pulled on a white T-shirt and a black sweater over the top of the jeans. I pulled on socks and then knocked the dried dirt from my sneakers and slipped them on. The thumping sound was coming from outside my window. When I finished getting dressed, I pushed the thin curtain aside and saw a woman astride a dapple gray mare inside the dirt arena, weaving her way around a course of barrels. Her body was pitched forward, urging her horse to go fast, and her long red hair streamed behind her.

I pulled my hair back into a ponytail and left my room. Last night, when we first arrived, the house was occupied. Between the music, the fire, the welcome wagon, and the late-night dinner, it felt social. But today, the place was quiet. I'd been dismissed before Sheriff Parker sought out Kathy to tell her about her husband, but I was sure the news had spread beyond the circle of people who'd been there last night.

A continental breakfast spread had been set up on the dining room table—apple fritters, buttermilk biscuits, fresh fruit, and four different kinds of juice. I poured a glass of OJ and downed it, feeling the effects of the sugar almost immediately. I grabbed a biscuit and went outside, expecting to find the rest of my party. I was wrong.

I walked around the side of the house to the horse arena and stood by the wooden fence to watch the woman on the horse. She urged her mare to go faster while she wove around barrels, knocking down one but not stopping. Eventually, she slowed down to a trot then a walk. It was then that she noticed me. She tugged on her reins and guided the horse to where I stood.

"If I'd known we had an audience, I wouldn't have knocked over that barrel." She glanced over her shoulder at the course.

"You were in the zone," I said. "You were fun to watch."

"Do you ride?"

I shook my head. "No, I'm just visiting. I'm Samantha."

"I'm Henna." She pointed to her hair. "Used to be brown. This way, people remember my name." She moved the reins to her left hand and leaned forward then pulled a pink bandana out of her back pocket and wiped her face clean of dirt. She stuffed the bandana back in her pocket.

"Do you work on the ranch?" I asked.

"Me? No." She pointed off to the tree line to the left. "I live over there. Joey lets me use the arena to practice, but I normally have to share it with the cowboys. Where is everybody?"

I stared up at her. Instead of answering, I asked a question of my own. "Was anybody out here when you arrived?"

"No, but that's not a problem. I know my way around the stables, and the owners trust me to put things back the way I found them when I'm done. Why?"

I didn't like being the one to spread gossip, but Henna didn't appear to know about last night, and me not saying anything felt like a manipulation of information.

"Do you know about Joey?" I asked.

"I heard something. It's a shame, but life goes on." She hopped down from her saddle and stroked the mane on her horse. "I feel bad for Kathy. She loves this place. I don't think she'd ever leave if Joey didn't force her."

"You're talking about the sale of the ranch," I said.

"Aren't you?"

"No," I said. "Joey is dead. He... died... last night."

Here's the thing nobody told you about finding murder victims. No matter how delicately you shared the news with strangers, you can't help the adrenaline burst of being the one who knew first. It wasn't a thrill like finding the perfect pair of shoes on the markdown rack or biting into a fresh-from-the-oven pizza. It was the opposite. Nausea tinged with numbness, with a halo of dizziness. It lasted for as long as it took for the recipient of the news to respond—horror, delight, curiosity, or nonchalance. It was in that moment that you slotted your interlocutor into a new column—gossip, friend, suspect. It was also in that moment that you realized you've just blown it for the police because the element of surprise will no longer be on their side.

Henna's eyes widened, and her pupils dilated. Her wind-whipped cheeks remained bright, two red spots on an otherwise freckled complexion. Her mouth opened and formed a perfect O, but no words came out.

"No wonder this place is a ghost town," she said. "What happened?"

And here's the part where you have to decide whether to tell the truth or lie? If you pretended you didn't know, the truth will come out, and when it did, your motives will be questioned. Maybe not by the police but by the lied-to party. That created animosity. If Nick's dad bought the ranch and Henna practiced in the arena on a daily basis, it might not be a good thing for me to have created a rift from the get-go.

"He was murdered in the stables," I said. "The local sheriff was out here last night. I don't know where everybody is this morning, but they were gone when I got up."

Whatever I expected her to say, it wasn't the response she gave. "Darn, girl, that's a tragedy." She flipped her red hair over her shoulder. The wind picked it up and tossed it behind her head. "I've got to cool down Strawberry for a few laps before I groom her. Can you stick around?"

I didn't have a chance to respond. A beat-up truck pulled down the dirty road and stopped a few yards from the arena. The driver climbed out. It was Cody.

"Hey, Henna," he called out. "You haven't been in the stables, have you?"

"I was about to head there now. What's up?"

"Off-limits, per Sheriff Parker." He glanced at me, and I nodded. He looked back at Henna. "You heard about Joey?"

"Samantha here told me."

Cody cast a scowl in my direction. "It's not public knowledge yet. Parker's keeping everybody here for the next few days until he gets a handle on what happened. Kathy's trying to figure out if she wants to sell the ranch at all. She's down at the sheriff's office, making a case for keeping the place running during the investigation, but the sheriff isn't having any of it."

"What about this weekend?" Henna asked. "It's been scheduled for months."

"Going to have to ask Kathy when she gets back, but it's not looking good."

He turned around and left.

"Not the friendliest cowboy, is he?" I asked.

"Don't mind Cody," she said. "He's worried about his job. Ever since Joey listed the ranch for sale, he's been on edge."

I stared at Cody as he climbed back into the truck and drove it down the dirt path and out of sight.

Henna stared after him too. "Guess that means I'm grooming Strawberry at home." She stroked the horse again, and he nuzzled his nose into her hand. "Nice meeting you, Sam. See you around."

She opened the latch on the gate and led Strawberry out, following the same dirt path Cody had driven.

No, I thought to myself. I was not going to think about the information I'd just learned, about Kathy not wanting to sell and about Cody being on edge about his future. I was not going to wonder about Henna living within walking distance or how many other neighbors had horses and could get here under cloak of night, effectively committing a murder and leaving no tracks.

Except they *would* leave tracks. If someone had ridden a horse here last night, the horse would have made tracks in the mud, tracks that might be visible today now that the mud had dried.

I turned around and looked down at the ground around my feet. Fresh tracks from a truck were visible. I walked slowly toward the entrance of the stables and searched the ground for hoof prints, or footprints, or cat prints, for that matter. The ground was smooth.

I realized while the ground had been muddy last night, the sky had been clear. We'd driven for two hours to get here, and there'd never been a drop of rain. I circled the stables, looking for anything out of the ordinary. And that was when I found the hose, hooked up to the outside of the building. A thin trickle of water came out from its end, dampening the ground by the side of the stables and making the ground squishy beneath my feet.

As soon as I realized what was happening, I backed up, but it was too late. The soles of my sneakers had flattened out the wet grass around the faucet, mashing any tracks that might have been made and leaving behind one set of footprints. Mine.

I wasn't going to think about why someone might have used the hose to make the ground in front of the stables muddy last night or why they might have been in such a hurry that they failed to turn off the hose properly today.

Who was I kidding? Of course I was.

The orange-and-white cat was sitting outside the front door when I returned. I joined him on the porch and pulled off my wet sneakers then set them next to the entrance. My hands were covered in dirt and grass, and lacking anything to wipe them on, I used Loncar's jeans, leaving behind muddy smudges on my thighs. Now I understood the bag of bandanas.

I opened the front door and let the cat in then followed him. He slunk over to the fire and flopped down on the braided rag rug in front of the hearth. I left him to warm himself while I went to my room for my book. Predictable behavior and all that. I returned with my Zane Grey, but the cat and I were no longer alone.

7

NOT UNFAMILIAR WITH MEDITATION

"Hɪ!" called out a blond woman in a floral prairie dress. "You must be Samantha."

"I am."

The woman had a peaceful air about her. She had curly blond hair loosely tied behind her neck. Loose curls framed her round face. She appeared to have been born with a peaches-and-cream complexion that was spotted by faint freckles across the bridge of her nose. Her eyebrows and eyelashes were blond, too, making her clear blue eyes and rosy cheeks stand out in contrast.

"Chef told me you stayed behind while the others went into town. I'm his wife, Mysti." She had been setting up a table of colorful trinkets and candles on the opposite side of the room, but she abandoned the display and approached me. "He told me what you went through last night. That's why I'm here."

"Because of the murder?"

"Because you shouldn't be alone," she said. Instead of shaking my hand like I anticipated, she put her arms around me and hugged. I'm not a particularly touchy-feely person, and I tensed under the unexpected gesture of intimacy, which surely did nothing to help sell the whole "I'm chill" vibe I was going for.

When we pulled apart, I noticed a small crease between Mysti's eyebrows, as if my tension was a source of concern. She reached for a crystal that dangled from a chain around her neck and worried the surface of it with her thumb and forefinger. I briefly wondered if that was an unconscious habit or if it worked like a genie in a bottle.

"When Chef told me what happened, I closed the shop and brought my event kit here." She gestured toward her display. "I can guide you through a meditation, if you'd like, or we can start with aromatherapy, if you prefer."

"I'm not... I don't... I'm sorry. You call your husband Chef?"

She giggled. "His name is Terry, but around here, people call him Chef. To make things easier, I got into the habit of calling Chef when I set up here."

"Do you set up a table here often?"

"When there are guests, yes. I'm a spiritual guide. I have a shop in town called Mystical Treasures, but I like to offer in-person services too. When I heard what happened to Joey, I thought it was more important to be here than there. People deal with tragedy in a number of ways, and sometimes, if they try to hold it in, they do long-term damage to their emotional side. I closed the shop for today, so I can work here until night. Have you ever practiced mindfulness and meditation?"

Now might be a good time to mention that I have, on occasion, been into things that others might call woowoo. I've done the breathing. I've set intentions. I've hung crystals over my doorway, followed the principles of feng shui in my living room, and burned sage to clear my energy. I believed in signs from the universe and moon power and the luck that came with a cricket finding its way into my house. I tried the life-changing magic of tidying up and even, for a short stint of time, had a life coach, all in the name of finding the thing that would bring me peace. What it brought me was a slightly annoyed husband (especially after he bruised his shin on the coffee table I'd moved). Two months ago, I packed up all of my tarot card decks and put the box in the attic. Maybe they would help the squirrel who got in through the hole in the roof to develop a third eye.

The thing was, I got the feeling that Nick was getting a little tired of hearing about the universe and the role it played in our futures. Plus, there'd been no discernable impact on our lives. I was still as curious as ever, and my curiosity still led me into situations that other people somehow avoided. My recent stress test indicated that I needed to find an outlet, but it also indicated that whatever outlets I'd sampled along the way hadn't done much in solving my problem. So you can understand how I might be conflicted over whether being here for Nick and his dad was at odds with hanging out with my new best friend.

"I'm not unfamiliar with meditation," I said cautiously, eyeing a fixture of hand-forged silver pendulums.

Mysti nodded. She stepped back and glanced down at the book in my hand. "I usually put on calming music while I set up. Will that bother you while you're reading?"

I glanced down at the book too. I doubted I was going to get absorbed in an adventure story about the American frontier while Mysti was across the room, but it no longer felt appropriate to excuse myself to go read in my room. I set the book on the sofa on top of the crocheted blanket and followed her to her table. "If you want an extra set of hands, I'm happy to help with your display."

By the time the men returned, Mysti had a veritable storefront in the lobby of the Down Home Ranch. This wasn't her first rodeo either. Any concerns I'd had about her wanting to push her brand of spiritualism on me dissipated when she slid a CD of soothing acoustic guitar music into a portable player. The sound system wasn't great, and the notes were on the tinny side of things, but it was better than silence or talking about the murder. I had to admit, Mysti had somehow tuned in to exactly what I needed. For the first time since arriving, I was almost sad that we'd be leaving before I had a chance to explore Mysti's brand of spiritualism.

The calming environment was shattered when the door burst open and a group of cowboys spilled in. I did a double take when I realized I knew one of those cowboys intimately. It was Nick.

Twenty-four hours on a ranch had been enough to take the edge off his day-to-day life running an existing shoedesign company and an emerging sneaker enterprise. A mink-brown cowboy hat covered his curly brown hair. One day of not shaving had left a shadow of stubble on his face. Like yesterday, his coloring was vivid, thanks to having spent the morning outdoors. His lips were deep red, and his cheeks were pink. His eyes, root-beer-barrel brown and framed by lashes that would make most women jealous, sparkled.

It wasn't just the hat, hair, and stubble that contributed to his cowboy appearance. He'd dressed in a faded blue shirt with pearl snap buttons and jeans that were held up by a rust-colored leather belt. His boots were coated in a layer of dirt, masking the bought-just-for-this-vacation appearance they'd had when he packed them. A purple bandana was knotted around his neck as if it were the most natural thing in the world.

"Hey, Kidd." He pulled off his hat, revealing curls matted down to his forehead. He held his hat in front of his chest and kissed me. My heartbeat picked up to a rate that would fail another stress test, and right before our lips met, a voice in my head asked, *Cowboy Nick?* and answered, *Yes, please.*

What can I say? The heart wants what the heart wants.

I didn't realize I was still kissing Nick until I heard someone clear their throat. We separated, and I glanced to the side. Angus, Cody, and a man I hadn't yet met were watching us. Mysti had left the room. Senior was petting the cat.

I patted Nick's chest, and he put his hat back on. If possible, his cheeks were even redder than mine. He shared an intimate smile with me, and I smiled shyly in return, as if we had a secret no one else knew.

"You get some sleep, kiddo?" Senior asked. "Junior wanted to wake you, but I said you could come with us tomorrow."

"Tomorrow? I thought we'd be leaving today." I looked back and forth between Nick and his dad for signs that I'd correctly read the situation.

"Leaving? We just got here," Senior said. "Did you think the Wild West was going to be agreeable? There's a reason it's called wild. I may be older than both of you, but I'm not dead yet. I could use a little wild in my life."

The color drained from Nick's face. His dad turned on his heel and stormed across the room.

"He's worse than you," Nick said.

"I resent that." We stood next to each other, watching Senior introduce himself to Mysti. "You were gone when I woke up. Where did you guys go?"

"Into town. Lulu eats a plant-based meat, so Chef had to go shopping for provisions."

As if on cue, Chef poked his head out of the kitchen. "Angus and Cody, can you give me a hand with this food haul?"

The two ranch hands entered the kitchen. A moment later, Cody was outside, walking toward the front of the ranch. An engine started, and the truck passed the same window on the way around back.

The third man, who I hadn't yet met, joined Senior and Mysti across the room.

"Who's that?" I asked Nick.

"Tully. He's the ranch manager."

"Why wasn't he here last night?"

"Who says he wasn't?"

"We didn't meet him."

"He lives in a cabin behind the stables."

"I didn't see any cabin."

"It's on the map."

"What map?"

Nick stepped in front of me, blocking my view of the rest of the people in the room. "Kidd, did you or did you not review the map of the ranch before we came here?"

"I told you, this is a relaxing vacation for me. I cleaned out the western section of the local bookstore and planned to catch up on my reading. The map I need for that is how to get from our room to the sofa."

"As long as you admit your lack of knowledge about the ranch layout is not some conspiracy to hide living quarters from you."

I narrowed my eyes. "Do Angus and Cody live in that cabin?"

"Cowboys live in the bunkhouse," Senior said from across the room. Until then, I hadn't realized anybody could hear our conversation. "I'm staying there tonight," he added.

Nick's emerging exasperation, previously directed toward me, shifted to his dad. "No, you're not."

"The heck I'm not. I don't run from a challenge. If I'm going to buy this ranch, I want to know what I'm buying. That bunkhouse is a part of the experience." Senior stormed into the hallway. A second later, the door slammed shut.

Nick and I stood close together, both of us staring at the hallway behind him. After another beat, I asked, "So, Tully was here last night?"

"Yes."

"Then he could have—" I caught myself right before I said the thing I wasn't going to say because I didn't want Nick to think I was getting involved.

"Samantha," Nick admonished. This time he turned his full attention from his dad to me.

"I'm just saying, Sheriff Parker might not know about him."

"Sheriff Parker has been the sheriff of Atlantic County for twenty-two years. He probably knows everybody who lives on this ranch."

"But he didn't say anything about Tully last night."

"It's not his job to share his investigation with you."

"I miss Loncar," I said, which was not nearly the non sequitur you might think.

"If memory serves, Detective Loncar didn't exactly treat you like a partner either."

I sighed. Nick wasn't wrong.

"Can you wrangle me an introduction to him?" I asked.

"Sure thing, pardner." Nick took my hand and led me to the ranch manager.

Before Nick had a chance to initiate the conversation, the red-haired man said, "You must be the little lady I've been hearing about. I'm Tully."

I seriously doubted that Nick or his father had described me as either little or ladylike, but I bit my tongue and held out my hand. "I'm Samantha."

He glanced at my outstretched hand and smiled as if he were amused by the gesture. He gripped it and shook. Calloused skin scratched my relatively soft hand, dwarfing it. I hadn't anticipated the roughness of his grip until too late. This was a man who used his hands every day, in circumstances I probably had never imagined.

"Tully manages the horses," Nick said. "He's going to take us out for a ride this afternoon."

"You didn't take the horses out this morning?" I asked, briefly looking at Tully but directing most of my attention to Nick. "The stables were empty when I went outside."

"Moved them last night," Regain said. "The sheriff wanted to go over the stables in the light of day, but horses aren't much for compliance with a sealed crime scene. If there was evidence to be found, one of them might have destroyed it by morning."

"Where did you take them?"

Something in Tully's initially friendly demeanor changed. His thick red eyebrows dropped down low over his blue eyes, hiding the top half of them behind hooded lids. "You know a lot about horses?" His question was direct and borderline accusatory, like he already knew the answer and was baiting me to misrepresent myself.

"Not really, though I'd love to learn."

"I'm not running a school here. You want to ride, I'll take you out. You want to learn, go to the library."

And before I could figure out what exactly I'd said to tick him off, he turned and stormed out the front door.

8

PEOPLE HAVE MURDERED FOR LESS

I wasn't the only one surprised by his actions. Nick and Senior flanked me, and all three of us stared at the closing door. Senior looked concerned. "I'll go make this right." And to my dismay, he followed Tully out the front door.

"You need to stop him," I said to Nick.

"From what? We're here for him. Tully is one of the employees. One of the most *trusted* employees. Joey's dad hired him when he was just a boy. He knows this place better than anybody else here."

"But he can't just expect people to climb on a horse and go for a ride without asking questions," I said. "What I asked him, that wasn't me getting involved. That was natural curiosity." Nick shot me a familiar look. "Okay, it was a little bit of me getting involved, but because your dad is thinking about buying the place and I'm not sure an open murder investigation hanging over the property is the best circumstances for a real estate transaction."

"Could be it gets him a better price if he wants it."

"If I didn't know your dad was above suspicion, that might sound like motive."

"*We* know he's above suspicion, but nobody else here does."

"Do you mean someone here might think your dad committed murder to get a land deal?"

"People have murdered for less."

BEFORE WE REGROUPED FOR LUNCH, we each went our separate ways. The group that had gone into town required more washing than I did, but hanging out by the fire with a book had not turned into the relaxing activity I'd thought it would be, so I grabbed my book and went out front to the porch. The arena was empty, and the barrels that Henna had raced around had been lined up at the end in a neat little row. The sun beamed down and warmed my face and hands despite the sixty-degree temperature. I kicked my feet out in front of me, tipped my head back, and closed my eyes. If someone had piped in the sound of seagulls, I might have believed I was on a beach in Jersey.

I knew that once I got Nick alone in our room, I would get the full play-by-play of his morning in town with Chef and Tully, and if anything unusual had happened, I would find out. I'd also tell him about Henna and Mysti, not because Nick had the same level of curiosity when it came to sniffing out murderers but because married couples shared the details of their days. And because, if I happened to rearrange the room furniture to improve the flow of our chi, I wanted Nick to understand why.

But that conversation was going to have to wait until later. A pickup truck rumbled onto the property and parked between the house and the stables. There had been a lot of coming and going since we arrived last night, but I should have expected this particular guest. It was Sheriff Parker. He held his thermos in one hand, and his open amber suede jacket revealed a holster and a badge both attached to his waistband.

He slammed his door and strode up to the house. "Mrs. Taylor," he said in greeting.

"Sheriff Parker," I said in return. I would have called him by the wrong name, too, but for now, I was on my best behavior. "What brings you back to the ranch?"

"Lunch."

I hadn't expected that answer, and I laughed out loud. He grinned at my response and picked up the orange-and-white cat and scratched his ears while he settled onto the porch swing next to me. The cat made a few turns on his lap before settling in. "Chef always makes too much food. I ran into the men in town today, and when Chef told me he was carving up a turkey for you all, I finagled an invite."

"Is 'finagled an invite' code for 'saw an opportunity to observe the various personalities who may have had access to a crime scene last night'?" I asked.

This time, Sheriff Parker laughed out loud, and like him, I met his outburst with a grin.

"That transparent, huh?" he asked.

"If you've already laid the groundwork, they probably won't see through your motives."

"But you did."

"I'm wired a little differently than the rest of them."

"Your father-in-law mentioned that. Said you have a history with this sort of thing."

I shifted my weight on the porch swing. "When did Senior tell you that?"

"This morning. If I didn't know any better, I'd say he was offering your services."

I'm not going to lie. The idea of helping was a little too big a carrot for me to ignore. "You want my help?"

The friendliness left Sheriff Parker's face, leaving behind leathery skin that was all creases and planes. "No, Ms. Kidd, I don't want your help. I'm conducting an investigation into a felony, using the tools made available to me by the state of New Jersey, and the last thing I need is an amateur sleuth playing Jessica Fletcher in my backyard."

What had started out as a friendly chat had quickly turned into something else, and I'd dropped my guard enough to be caught unprepared for the assault.

"I wish you all the best in your investigation, Sheriff.

I'd hate to think my father-in-law has put his life at risk by choosing to trust you and your New Jersey toolbox." I stood up, rocking the swing and waking the cat in the process. "I'm going inside to check on lunch."

"Save me a seat," he called behind me.

Lunch, it turned out, was something of a production. Three freshly sliced turkeys sat on platters along the length of the table alongside several hot-from-the-oven loaves of sourdough bread, plates of lettuce, and condiment trays of mustard and relish. Sliced apples and pears were fanned out in circles, and large bowls of potato and macaroni salad were stationed between them. Sheriff might have been wrong about my involvement, but he was right about Chef making too much food. At my last count, there were eight of us at the ranch, though the morning had already taught me that people had a way of coming out of the woodwork.

Around the table sat Senior, Nick, Mysti, Cody, Tully, Sheriff Parker, and Angus. Despite the efforts Chef had gone to for Lulu and her plant-based diet, she and her husband, Billy, weren't present.

"Are Billy and Lulu joining us?" I asked.

"They're still in town," Angus said.

"Just as well," Chef added as he set a giant Waldorf salad on the table. "The market doesn't stock vegan turkey breasts. Sure wish they'd told me ahead of time of her dietary restrictions. I placed an order, but the food won't be ready for pickup until tomorrow."

"What about Kathy?" I asked. No one answered.

Last night, I'd been concerned for her, for how she might take the news of her husband's murder. But a conversation I'd almost forgotten came back to me, a conversation between Angus and Henna, the barrel racer. He'd said Kathy was in town meeting with Sheriff Parker, making a case to keep the ranch open during his investigation. That didn't sound like the actions of a distraught wife.

I rephrased my question. "Is Kathy joining us?" I directed my attention to Angus. He was across the table from me, in the process of spearing several slices of turkey for his sandwich, but my question appeared to give him pause.

"Kathy went into town," Cody said. "Official ranch business." He picked up his own sandwich and bit into it noisily, thanks to the crisp bacon and the iceberg lettuce he'd added. "I reckon she won't be back until after dark."

There was more to what Cody said than what Cody said. The fact that Kathy had left the ranch at all surprised me, and the fact that she had official ranch business to conduct less than twelve hours after her husband was found murdered in a stall surprised me more. If anything happened to Nick, I probably wouldn't get out of bed for six months.

Already, I'd gotten the feeling that those of us at the ranch were divided into two groups—employees and guests. Senior and Nick appeared to have gained some backstage access, but I'd been relegated to the guest column. I was used to being the person on the inside (mostly because I put myself there, but still). I didn't like the way I'd been treated like a helpless female from the moment we'd arrived, and I didn't like being on the outside with my nose pressed up against the glass.

I held my knife and fork over my plate and waited for Angus—or anybody—to add something to the conversation. But the table went silent, save for the sounds of utensils scraping plates and crunchy food being consumed. Despite my love of food, I was without appetite, thanks to my late breakfast. I slathered a slice of freshly baked bread with butter and bit into it while observing the rest of the folks. To anyone else, this would seem like a group that had worked up an appetite after spending a day on the ranch, but not to me. I couldn't help think that someone at this very table had secrets that had led to last night's crime.

And as I observed Sheriff Parker across the table, I realized I wasn't the only one with questions. The chatty sheriff was there in mind and body, but based solely on the untouched plate of food in front of him, his reasons for being at the table had less to do with food than mine.

9

NOT USED TO NOT HELPING

By the time lunch had finished, I determined my best way to infiltrate the group was through Mysti and Chef. I didn't know jack squat about horses, aside from what I'd read in Trixie Belden books when I was growing up, but I knew about mindfulness, and I knew about food. If playing those cards was going to make me some friends on the ranch, I was going to brush up on *Hoyle's Rules of Games* and double down on my aces.

It would be easy enough to separate Mysti from the rest of the group. When the men stood and moved to the leather seating arrangement by the fire, she excused herself and went back to her display of crystals. I was left behind, surrounded by empty plates. Chef came out of the kitchen to check on us, and when he saw the vacated seats, he asked if I wanted something else to eat.

"No, thank you," I said. "I'm not as hungry as the rest of them."

"Ranch work builds up an appetite." He glanced at my plate, which still had half a turkey sandwich along with a helping of potato salad. "You should go out this afternoon. The ranch is prettiest at sunrise and sunset. Dinner won't be until seven thirty, so you've got plenty of time to work off lunch."

"Do you ride?"

"Not as much as I'd like, but I manage."

"When?" I asked. Chef looked confused by my question. "You were making breakfast this morning when the rest of them were out. Now you're here making lunch. When do you ride?"

"For recreation? Early. And late. I'm up early each day to collect eggs from the chickens and gather whatever other resources I can from the land. My job keeps me in the kitchen most of the day, so I enjoy the early-morning solace. When I'm not prepping food, I'm in town buying supplies, like I was today. But don't let that fool you. After I clear the table and pack up the leftovers, I've got a few spare hours before I start dinner. And after dinner's packed up, I'm free for the night unless the group calls for something special after dark." His eyes cut from me to my plate again, and he surveyed the table. He kept his hands folded behind his back. "Are you sure you don't want anything else?"

"I'm fine," I said.

I felt two hands on my shoulders, and I looked up, expecting to see Nick. Instead, it was Mysti. Her long hair was swept to the side, with loose curls spilling down over her shoulder. Her crystal necklace swung forward and tapped my head. She massaged my shoulders ever so slightly, working at tense muscles with her thumbs. I felt myself start to relax despite the surprise of her touch.

"What my husband is too polite to tell you is that he can't clear the table until everybody leaves."

"Mysti," Chef said sharply.

"You're not being fair to Samantha. You took her husband and father-in-law into town for the food shop. They probably learned a thing or two about how the ranch runs from spending time with you. Samantha doesn't know anything about life on the ranch. She deserves a peek behind the curtain too." She hiked her dress up to her knees and straddled the bench next to me, revealing her ivory suede cowboy boots as she did so. "If you want something else, it's Chef's job to make it. If you want to graze the food that's already out, that's fine, too, but he won't clear the table until all seats have been vacated."

I was horrified by my lack of social awareness. I jumped up from the table and grabbed the bowl of potato salad. "I'll help you."

Mysti put her hand on mine. "No, you won't. That's his job."

"I'm not used to not helping." With my hand still on the bowl, I looked from her face to Chef's. He nodded. I set the bowl back down on the table. "What exactly am I supposed to do?"

"Come with me," Mysti said. "It's about time you

found out what the rest of your group already knows." She grabbed my hand and pulled me toward the door.

It didn't matter what secrets I was about to learn. For the first time since we'd arrived, someone wanted me to do something, and that was enough.

By the time Mysti led me out the front door, the men had moved from inside by the fireplace to the arena, where they stood with arms hanging over the fence. Mysti didn't even acknowledge them. She walked past them, the stables, and a small cabin on the opposite side of the stables that I hadn't seen the night before, moving directly toward the tree line. The loose-fitting fabric of her prairie dress blew around her legs, occasionally clinging to her calves. The cowboy boots I'd purchased at Boot Barn last week were black leather with ivory stitching. They were still in my room, packed underneath the books I'd planned to read. I'd purchased them under duress. A blog about what to pack for a week on a ranch had put *decent cowboy boots* on the top of the list, but in terms of footwear purchases, I would have much preferred something with a red sole.

Mysti's boots were ivory suede with colorful floral embroidery. She didn't seem to care that dirt swirled around her ankles, discoloring the suede and muting the pink and blue flowers stitched onto the leather. She used long strides, as though confident that she could handle anything that might be in her path.

I jogged a few steps to catch up to her and dropped into stride. There was a purpose to her forward momentum. This wasn't a casual stroll. She didn't say anything at first, but I matched her pace. It felt good to stretch my legs.

Once we reached the tree line, Mysti turned to the left and stopped. She shielded her eyes, already hidden behind shaded aviator sunglasses, and stared back at the ranch. I mimicked her behavior, but unprepared as I was, I had to squint. This was the farthest I'd been from the property, and from here, the buildings appeared small, like a reproduction of a ranch at model scale. The main house looked empty. Sheriff Parker's truck was gone, but the other beat-up truck, the one that had transported the supplies from Chef's shopping trip in town, was parked between the house and the stables. The group of men still stood outside the arena. I counted Senior, Nick, and the two cowboys. Two redheaded people, Tully and Henna, were mounted on horses inside the small fence. They trotted around in a circle, Henna behind Tully, their horses seeming to have worked out a choreography that allowed them to move in tandem. I hadn't thought too much about it when I'd met them, but together, even from a distance, it seemed relatively obvious that they were related.

"Tully and Henna," I said. "Father, daughter?"

"Uncle, niece," Mysti said. "Her father died when she was a little girl, and her mother left. Tully might as well be her father. He raised her from when she was three. First put her on a horse when she was four and entered her in her first competition when she was five."

"She seems like a natural."

"She won her first blue ribbon at six." Mysti turned away from me. "We've all been proud of her. A lot of people learn about the ranch after seeing her race at the weekend rodeo. But Henna's not six anymore. She's a grown woman. Tully made sure she knows her way around a horse, but he hasn't done a lot to make sure she knows her way around people."

"She seems well-adjusted enough to me," I said.

"You met her?"

"This morning. Before you arrived. The men were in town, and I wanted to... explore the ranch." I remembered exactly what I'd been thinking when I went outside, and it had nothing to do with exploring the ranch and everything to do with exploring the stables for clues. I felt heat rush to my cheeks, and I welcomed the relief of the wind snapping around us. "Henna was practicing."

"That can't be," she said. "Chef said the stables were off-limits."

"Where did Tully move the horses?"

"He left them tethered to the fence gate while Sheriff Parker went over the inside of the stables. The sheriff asked if Tully could hold off on grooming the horses until this afternoon. That meant not saddling them up, not giving them a morning workout."

I turned away from Mysti and stared at the group across the field. None of them had said they took the horses out, but they'd implied it. Or maybe I'd jumped to conclusions based on their ruddy complexions and their dirt-coated attire. It was one more thing that hadn't been as it seemed, and I realized how easy it was to jump to wrong conclusions here on the ranch.

"What about Tully? How's he with people? I heard he's worked on this ranch since before Joey and Kathy took it over."

If Mysti was troubled by my line of questioning, she didn't show it. "Tully's been here longer than any of us. In some ways, Tully *is* the Down Home Ranch. It's sad to think of this place without him."

"Did he quit? Where's he going?"

Mysti pulled her hair back and held it behind her head. The wind picked up, and strands of blond hair snapped around her cherubic face. "You must know the ranch is being sold as a property only," she said. "When Joey told the staff he'd listed the place for sale, he advised them to start looking for employment elsewhere. Angus and Cody will pick up work at one of the neighboring ranches. There's always a need for cowboys. But there are only so many opportunities for stable managers in the area, and most ranches already have someone who has been in their employ for decades. Tully's too old to start over, but he's not equipped for anything else."

"He wouldn't take work as a cowboy?"

"Cowboy work is demanding. This ranch makes its income from vacationing groups like yours, but others don't think that's right. They breed cattle or break horses that get sold off at auction. This place suits Tully, but another one won't."

I turned away from Mysti and looked back out at the arena. Tully and Henna had dismounted their horses. Tully's was tethered to the arena gate. Henna stood off to the side talking, still holding the reins to her horse. Two additional people had joined the group—Billy and Lulu, both mounted on horseback. Hail, hail, the gang's all here.

Mysti's and my conversation lapsed into silence as we watched the ranch hands carry a wooden hurdle out into the middle of the dirt arena. Lulu, who last night had looked every bit the vacationing tourist in her brand-new western wear, appeared to be one with her horse. She rode around the perimeter of the arena, first at a trot then a gallop. Lulu stood in her stirrups and urged her horse to go faster and faster. Her hair was like a banner flapping behind her. She was up, out of the saddle, hands tight on the reins, moving with her horse as one. Together they approached the hurdle in the center of the arena, and I watched helplessly as her horse's foot caught on the barrier and tossed Lulu over his head and onto the ground.

10

TROUBLE ON THE RANCH

MYSTI GATHERED FISTFULS OF FABRIC BY HER THIGHS AND took off running. I followed. We were far enough from the arena that we'd be the last to join the group, but that didn't stop us. Lulu's horse, scared by the sudden chaos surrounding the accident, headed for the arena gates. He favored one of his feet, indicating an injury sustained while in the ring. Mysti stopped running as she approached the horse and made clicking noises with her tongue. She slowly reached out for the dangling reins, stroked the horse's mane, and spoke to him quietly.

"Stay with her," Mysti said to me. She held out the reins.

I backed away and held my hands up. "I don't know anything about horses."

"Hold her reins securely and talk to her in a calm voice. I'll send Tully over to check her out. She's spooked, but she's hurt. Tully needs to inspect her and find out what caused the accident."

There was no time for me to beg off from the task at hand. I took Strawberry's reins nervously. Mysti handed me a red bandana she pulled out of a pocket on her dress then left me and strode toward the group clustered around Lulu.

Lulu was sitting up. Cody was on one side of her, and Tully was on the other. I didn't think anybody should consider moving her, but they did. With perfect timing, they lifted her to her feet and draped her arms around each of their shoulders. With the assistance of the cowboys, she made it to the bench outside the stables, appearing to put one foot in front of the other while the bulk of her body weight was supported by the men who flanked her. Her husband, Billy, took the seat next to her and kept his arm around her protectively.

My heartbeat pounded in my ears, thanks to the short dash across the field to reach the group. Even though I was in sneakers, it hadn't been easy. The terrain was rough and still damp in places, with each step carrying the potential for a twisted ankle or another fall into the mud. Despite the wind keeping the temperatures on the cooler side, the hot sun bore down on me. At first, it felt good, but my skin tingled, and I feared I was getting sunburned.

I wasn't comfortable veering far from the arena with a horse in tow, but from where I stood, I heard Tully call out instructions to Henna. "Go into town and find Kathy. Tell her we need her back at the ranch."

Henna mounted her horse in a graceful motion and kicked his flanks with the heels of her boots, taking off for the entrance to the ranch. Cody, the flirtatious cowboy, untethered Tully's horse from the gate. I thought he was going to follow Henna, but he led the horse away from the arena and around the back of the stables. The horse pulled at the restraints, but Cody kept a firm grip. There was nothing flirtatious about his behavior.

By the time she disappeared around the corner, Chef had joined us from inside. He sat on the other side of Lulu while Tully squatted in front of her, holding her hands and talking to her in a soothing tone of voice. Mysti came out of the house with a bottle of water. She uncapped it and handed it to Lulu, who held it in both hands but didn't take a sip. In a parallel way, this was like watching the employees in the arena. Each person handled their role while not interfering with another, as if this very situation had been choreographed long ago and they were all performing their parts.

While the employees of the ranch attended to Lulu, Nick joined me. He reached out and stroked Strawberry's mane, pulled a sugar cube out of a pocket on his shirt, and held it out for her. She tipped her head down, sniffed it, and ate it from his palm.

"Good girl," he said gently. He kept his hand moving over her mane, his back to the group by the bench.

"Lulu was just thrown off a horse," I said to Nick,

working to keep my voice at a calm, even level so as not to spook the dapple gray mare in question. "Shouldn't someone get a doctor? Shouldn't she be X-rayed or get an MRI?"

"Maybe someone did call a doctor."

While Nick watched Strawberry, I surveyed the group, this time picking out Senior on the fringes. He watched Tully and Chef with the same concern that I felt. It wasn't our place to tell the employees how to handle this accident, but the way they responded, as if containment were more important than medical care, raised massive suspicions about what transpired when tourists weren't around. Maybe we'd been granted a peek behind the inner workings of the ranch, but I didn't think they wanted us to see how easily ranch merriment could turn to tragedy for the second time in twenty-four hours.

Lulu's accident had temporarily made me forget all about the murder, but now, I drew connections between the two events. Joey had been killed just last night. Were these two incidents isolated, or was there a connection? And if so, why? Was someone making trouble on the ranch?

The accident had changed the energy of the afternoon. Whatever fun and games had been transpiring in the arena, they'd been traded for a more somber atmosphere. If anybody had noticed the three of us standing along the sidelines, watching the rest of the employees care for Lulu, they would have told us to stay out of the way, maybe even to go inside, but they didn't, so we didn't. I was painfully aware of my role as spectator and not helper, though even I could tell the last thing Lulu needed was another person attending to her needs.

Tully peeled away from the group and approached Nick. "I'm going to need some help resetting the arena."

Nick nodded. "Wait here while I tether Starlight and Jupiter."

"What about Strawberry?" I asked.

Tully glanced at me and back at Nick. "What did Mysti tell you to do?"

"Stay with her until Tully was able to take a look at her foot."

"Then stay with her until Tully is able to take a look at her foot."

"But—"

It didn't matter what I was about to say. My protest landed on Tully's back as he walked away.

"Yes, I see the way he treats you, too, but no, we're not going to talk about it," Nick said in acknowledgement of Tully's dismissive attitude toward me. "Not right now."

I appreciated his intuitiveness, though I still felt sidelined by Tully's treatment.

Nick tipped his hat back and stared after Tully. "This is a different world than the one we're used to. I have to believe there's a reason they act like they act." He leaned down and kissed me briefly. "Until we know what's going on here, try not to rock the boat."

I nodded.

Cody returned from behind the stables, wearing

heavy leather gloves. He waved Nick over to join him by the hurdle, and together they disassembled the rig and carried it away. Moments later, Cody drove a truck with a drag attached past the white gates and initiated the process of grooming the arena. For a few minutes, Nick and I stood next to each other, silently watching Cody drive the truck in large circles, tilling the dirt behind him and leaving a smooth surface in his wake. It was the ranch version of a Zamboni.

I thought back to Lulu's accident and how it had played out. She'd been the center of attention. The ranch employees, Nick, and his dad had all been gathered around the gate to watch Henna and Tully perform. Lulu and Billy, who'd been absent from the group lunch, had returned in time to perform for the group too. But Henna hadn't been jumping hurdles. She and Tully had been racing around the perimeter, showing off their speed and mastery as well as the trust they each had with their horses. That wasn't what Lulu had displayed. Something was odd about her accident, but I couldn't work out what it was.

I stroked the dapple gray mare's mane. "You were there. It's too bad you can't tell me what happened." The horse nuzzled my hand, and I made a mental note to add sugar cubes to my pockets like Nick had. "I bet you'd tell me if you could."

An unexpected gust of wind blew through the trees, rattling their dry leaves and sending them into the air. Strawberry stepped to the left and stumbled. I made sure my grip on her reins was tight and stepped a few feet away. Strawberry moved again, this time bending her front left leg and holding it above the ground.

I was not so foolish to think I could diagnose a horse's injury, but it seemed as though something was wrong with Strawberry's foot. I was so absorbed in what this might mean that I didn't hear Tully come up behind me.

"Go into the house. Storm's coming."

"She's hurt. It's her foot."

"I'll handle Strawberry."

I gripped the reins more tightly, suddenly concerned by what handling an injured horse might mean. "What are you going to do?" I asked, feeling an unexpected surge of protectiveness toward her. I might not know much about horses, but I knew that, like the cat, Strawberry had accepted my presence despite my city-mouse aura.

"I'm going to get that saddle off her before she puffs up and makes it darn near impossible to release, then I'm going to give her a bath and a handful of carrots. When she's fully relaxed, I'm going to check out her feet and ankles and make sure she didn't sustain any serious injuries when she tripped." He put his hand on her mane and stroked her lovingly, and no matter what conclusions I'd jumped to, it was obvious Tully cared for her deeply. "Her jumping days might be over, but she's got a lot more love to give."

I released the reins, and Tully led her away from the arena to the stables. Cody drove in slow circles over the dirt, tilling the ground of the track and leaving behind a consistent bed of dirt. Nick said something to Angus that I couldn't hear, thanks to the machine's engine, and he pointed to the house. I twisted and looked in the direction of his arm. Kathy had returned.

Cody stared at the porch for a moment while the till's engine idled, and he put the truck in park and climbed down. He said something to Nick, who nodded and climbed onto the machine. Angus strode toward the fence, swung one leg then the other over it, and walked toward Kathy.

Now that I was free from assignments, I followed Nick. He was familiarizing himself with the controls of the till.

"Do you know what you're doing?" I asked. If so, Nick had skills I'd never known about.

"It's like a riding mower." He grabbed the shift and tried to move it into another position. The gears grinded, emitting a sharp screech, and the till drove backward two feet. Nick let go, and the sound subsided, replaced by the hum of the engine. "I'll figure it out in a second."

Under normal circumstances, I would offer suggestions or maybe even a theory on how to make the ranch equipment work based on nothing but my observations and general belief that I had been put on this earth to solve other people's problems. If Nick and I couldn't figure out how to work it together, I would get someone from the ranch and put it on them. Their negligence in telling us what to do or how to do it was the root of the problem, not our inability to figure things out.

But I'd been told too many times since we'd arrived to stay out of it, to leave the jobs to the people assigned to them, to mind my own business, and to just sit back and relax. I'd been made to feel that there was no place for me here aside from the sofa in front of the fire or the bed behind closed doors. And a thin trickle of resentment had started building, at war with my need to support Nick and his dad in this new venture. I didn't like having my hands tied, but that was how I felt.

Nick finally succeeded in putting the machine in drive. He turned the wheel hard to the right and made a circle in the dirt then drove toward the entrance. And as the cloud of dirt by my sneakers settled, I realized that while I'd been in everybody's way my first day on the ranch, right now, I was exactly where I needed to be to spot a small metallic item embedded in the arena floor.

Maybe Strawberry was too old to handle hurdle jumping in the arena, but that wasn't what had caused her injury. It was a long gold nail. Like the one Joey had the night we first arrived.

I'd found Joey's body in the stables, but his nail was lying in the middle of the arena. It begged one very important question.

What exactly had transpired out here last night?

11

THE DO-NOTHING-THANK-YOU-MA'AMS

I DROPPED DOWN TO MY HANDS AND KNEES AND CLAWED AT the compressed ground surrounding the embedded nail until I was able to free the nail with my fingers. A cloud of dirt puffed up and got caught in my throat. I coughed a few times, trying to get a decent breath, and pressed Mysti's bandana over my mouth. By the time I finished my task, my fingernails were clogged with dirt. I smacked my hands together, stood, and wiped my hands on Loncar's jeans. I smoothed the bandana out on the ground and set the nail into the center of it then wrapped the faded cotton around it.

Once I'd seen the nail, it was an easy decision to pick it up, but now that I had it in my possession, I was less clear on who I should tell about it. Tully made the most sense. He oversaw the stables and cared for the horses. If I was right and the nail belonged to Joey, then either Joey lost it before he was murdered or the person who murdered him dropped it after killing him. Either scenario made Lulu's accident seem like just that—an accident.

Unless the person who had dropped the nail had a reason for wanting the ranch to continue to suffer. But who would want the ranch to crash and burn? It was already for sale. The Down Home Ranch would change hands in a matter of time, and the likeliest scenario was that it would never again be what it was now. Trouble at the ranch would deter one very specific segment of the public—prospective buyers. And who else would have benefited from a sale? Joey, who was now dead.

If I was right, then I needed to find the person most likely to block the sale. And from what I'd learned from Mysti, that person was Tully. That alone was enough to keep me from showing him what I'd found.

I put the wrapped-up nail into the back pocket of my jeans and walked to the house. Kathy stood inside, talking to Cody. He had his hand on her arm, as if he were comforting her.

Kathy was the one person who should have felt the weight of the two tragedies, but she didn't seem like a woman who had just lost her husband. She nodded and put her hand over Cody's hand on her arm. There was something intimate about the gesture, as if these two people were comfortable with each other's touch. I didn't know if they were aware of my presence, but if they were, they did nothing to keep me from eavesdropping on their conversation.

"Call Sheriff Parker," Kathy said. "Tell him what happened."

"You don't think this was connected to—" Cody started, but Lulu cut him off.

"I think Lulu was an inexperienced jumper who had an accident, but I told the sheriff that we would cooperate with his investigation. This is me cooperating with his investigation."

Cody put his free hand under Kathy's chin and raised her face so she was looking directly at him. "You sure?"

"I am. Thank you for taking care of it."

Cody left the room.

"How is Lulu?" I asked, alerting Kathy to my presence. If she was embarrassed by discovering that I'd observed her with Cody, she didn't show it.

"She shows no sign of injury, but I'll feel better after a doctor has a chance to give her an exam."

"Is someone on their way? She probably shouldn't be moving around after a fall like that."

"I hope so. After Henna found me in town, she went to the clinic to alert the staff that we'll need someone here."

I almost hated to ask the question on the tip of my tongue, but a nod is as good as a wink to a blind horse. "Is there anything I can do to help?"

"No," she said. "You're a guest. I shouldn't even be talking to you about our problems."

I'd had just about enough of the do-nothing-thank-you-ma'ams. "You know that's not true." I studied her face, looking for signs that I'd offended her. She studied me in return. If there was anything more than curiosity behind her steel-gray eyes, she did a good job of hiding it.

I gave the silence between us one beat more than was comfortable and continued. "I'm not just a guest. I'm part of the family looking to buy your ranch. If the sale happens, I'll have an integral role in running the place." (Between you and me, that was a bit of a bluff, but she didn't need to know that.) "The more I know about your day-to-day, the more effectively I'll be able to transition into that role and keep things running without a hitch."

"I thought your father-in-law was the prospective buyer," she said with a trace of accusation in her voice. "I thought he wanted to buy the ranch as an investment and hire a team to oversee it as a resort property, not move your family here to take over the day-to-day."

Crap. Of course Senior had shared his ideas with the current property owners. Why, when everybody else seemed to want to keep secrets, did I have to be with the party who told the truth? It was like running a campaign for a clean politician. I was without both power *and* leverage.

"Senior is keeping his options open."

"Isn't he in his seventies?"

"That's my point." I glanced around to make sure nobody (and by nobody, I meant Nick and his dad) could hear me, and I lowered my voice. "He thinks he's capable. You and I both know there's more to the job than checking in guests. I can help paint an accurate picture of the job if I know what's involved, but if your staff continues to shut me out of the daily operations, I'm at a loss."

Behind me, the door to the ranch opened. I heard the scrape of the hinges and felt the blast of cool air on my back. Kathy, too short to look over my shoulder, tipped her head and looked around my arm. I didn't want to encourage her to get distracted, so I kept my back to the door and my focus on her. If she left me hanging, it wasn't because I hadn't laid out a rational explanation for why I should know things. It was because she had unspoken reasons for leaving me in the dark.

Unfortunately, we were interrupted anyway. "Kathy. A moment?" Tully said behind me.

Kathy glanced at me. She moved to the seating area where Tully stood. He held his hat in his hands and looked at her sheepishly, as if he had bad news for which he was somehow responsible. The fire crackled next to them, removing any chance I had at eavesdropping. I stood, alone, in the middle of the room, wanting to help troubleshoot the problems that were cropping up but unsure how.

The longer I stood there, the more conspicuous I felt. Chef came out of the kitchen with his hands full. He set two plates on the table and went back through the saloon doors, returning with two bowls. I migrated toward the table to investigate. In terms of distractions, this was effective. Vessels of popcorn sat next to plates of brownies and Rice Krispies treats embedded with M&M's. I hovered nearby.

"Help yourself," Chef said. "We've got more than enough for the group here."

I stuffed a handful of popcorn into my mouth. I expected it to be salty, but it was sweet. Immediately, I grabbed a napkin and spit it back out.

"Kettle corn," Chef said. "It's seasoned with sugar instead of salt."

"That's just wrong," I said. "Don't you ever just make it with butter, like at the movies?"

"The kettle is the ranch way, but if you want, I'll make up a batch just for you."

I scanned the table. "I'll make do." I grabbed a kernel of popcorn and tried again. This time I managed to swallow it, but still, I was not a fan. "People actually like this?"

"Yup. We normally go through garbage bags of the stuff during a sing-along. I start making it a few days ahead of time, but with the cancellation this weekend, we'll be eating kettle corn for breakfast."

"What is this word 'sing-along'?" I asked, happy to have found someone willing to chat with me.

Chef grinned. "On Saturday nights, we host entertainment. In the summer months, it's dressage or rodeo competitions. When the weather turns cooler, we bring things inside. Kathy books local musicians, and we throw a party. It's an introduction to the ranch for a lot of people, and some of them go on to book stays here. Best use of advertising I've seen."

"Aren't you competing with clubs in town?" I asked.

"Yes and no. Kathy and Joey saw a drop-off in visitors in September and came up with a winter agenda. She books the entertainment, Tully serves beer for tips, and Mysti does spiritual readings from the lobby."

"What about Cody and Angus?"

"They mingle with the crowd. You'd be surprised how many of the ladies like to flirt with a cowboy."

I remembered the unexpected flutter I felt each time I saw Nick in his Stetson. I didn't correct Chef aloud, but I wasn't surprised at all.

Chef went back into the kitchen and returned with potato chips and cheese puffs. He set them on the table and arranged them in a row down the center.

Chef left me grazing from the table and went back into the kitchen. When he returned, I asked about the cancellation. "Did Sheriff Parker tell Kathy to cancel the party for Saturday night?"

"No. In fact, he released the crime scene and said she could return to regular operations."

"Then she canceled because of Lulu's accident?"

"Kathy wasn't the one to cancel. It was the entertainment. The Yee-Haws have been on the schedule for months, but they notified her this morning that they weren't going to make it. Sent an email to say their manager double-booked them and apologized for the inconvenience."

"Did they have to refund a booking fee or something?"

"No. The performers get a cut of the take at the door. It incentivizes them to promote to their fan base and draw more people to the event."

"So the Yee-Haws are out nothing, but Kathy's got a hole on her promotional calendar. Does that happen frequently?"

"Nope. This is a good gig for a band looking to raise their exposure. Get in front of a lot of people who may never have heard of you. We're about an hour south of Asbury Park and an hour north of Wildwood. Sometimes scouts will show up to find new acts."

My mind raced with questions and answers. It felt like one more nail hammered into the coffin of the Down Home.

"Has news of Joey's murder spread?" I asked. As soon as the question was out of my mouth, I realized Chef was a veritable stranger, and asking him questions about a murder on the property might not be part of his regular canon of conversation.

"Nothing in the paper, but these things have a way of spreading. Kathy went into town this morning to try to scare up a replacement act, but Lulu's accident brought her back to the ranch before she made any progress."

I felt a familiar buzzing sensation. It was familiar because it was linked with my internal need to solve problems. Like a mystic with a third eye, I saw a way forward. Maybe it was the proximity to Mysti's display of crystals?

"Thanks, Chef," I said. "You just gave me an idea."

I tossed the rest of my Rice Krispies treat into a nearby trash bin and reached into my pocket for my already-filthy bandana. I'd forgotten about the gold nail from the arena, and when I opened the bandana, the nail fell to the wooden floor with a clank. Kathy and Tully looked over at me, and I stooped down and scooped it up, hopefully before either one of them saw it.

I quickly rewrapped the nail and kept it in my hand. I strode across the floor to Kathy and Tully, making no secret of my approach.

"Excuse me," I said to them. "Kathy, I heard about the Yee-Haws. I know you... you both," I added, including Tully, "have wanted to keep me from helping out in the running of the ranch. And I can appreciate that. But I have to ask. Is Saturday's party absolutely necessary? In light of everything that's happened since we arrived?"

"You don't understand," Kathy said. "We're usually booked full with parties and equestrian performances. That's business. Saturday night is a way for us to entertain the staff while also publicizing the ranch. A lot of people come out here for the first time on a Saturday night, and the people who come to us now will be the same ones who book their events in the spring. We can't afford to miss a weekend, especially if we don't find a buyer."

It was the opening I needed. "Then let me help.

Before you officially cancel Saturday night's event, give me the rest of the afternoon to go into town and find a replacement act."

I didn't say it was the least I could do, because so far, they hadn't wanted me to do anything. There was absolutely no reason for them to turn down my offer. I wasn't asking to make dinner, or exercise horses, or mop the floor, or collect eggs for breakfast. But this offer, this was more than a way for me to help out. It had the appearance of getting me out of the way.

Kathy turned to Tully. "What do you think?" She didn't appear confident in me or my suggestion, but she also didn't seem to have come up with an immediate reason to reject it.

"It *would* solve a certain cash-flow problem," Tully said. He scratched his red hair and left a small chunk sticking straight out on the side. "Your husband can drive my truck into town. I gassed it up before your party arrived. I can't spare Cody, but Angus knows a lot of people. He can—"

"No," I said quickly. "I'll go with Nick. Consider this problem solved."

The two of them looked at me with more than a little skepticism, which may have been warranted. I didn't know anything about booking a musical act for a calendar opening three days away.

But I knew somebody who could maybe, possibly, help. And all it would take was a covert phone call and another favor to be returned at a later date.

12

COWBOY COLLECTIBLES

"You said we'd do what?" Nick asked. To his credit, he waited until we were in the truck to ask, but that was mostly because I didn't tell him why we were going into town until we were in the truck.

"Calm down," I said. "I have a plan."

After offering to solve Kathy's entertainment deficit, I'd snuck away to my room and made a phone call, which went something like this:

"I need your help." Pause. "I'm at the ranch, and their musical entertainment for Saturday night canceled. I thought you might know somebody because you're more connected to this world than I am. I know it's a lot to ask, but there's a murder involved, and it might have something to do with the sale of the ranch, which puts Nick Sr. in the crosshairs. Plus, it wouldn't be the worst thing to have you here as backup."

My request was met with silence. I wasn't unfamiliar

with Detective Loncar's silences—who did you think I called?—but usually we were face-to-face and I could infer enough from his body language to predict his response. (Except in that one case where he cuffed me and carted me off to the police station, but that was back before we'd established a working relationship.)

"Can you help me?" I added.

"Go into town. Find a bar called the Boot Strap. Talk to Maverick. Tell him Charlie Loncar sent you."

"Charlie? Not Detective?"

"I'm not a detective anymore."

"You're a private investigator, though, admittedly, Private Investigator Loncar doesn't exactly roll off the tongue."

"Use my name. Maverick will know who I am."

"Okay. Good. Sure. On it."

"Ms. Kidd, I don't need to tell you to stay out of the investigation, do I?"

"I've been the picture of cooperation. Sheriff Parker will probably deputize me by the time we leave."

Loncar cleared his throat.

"The truth is, I couldn't interfere if I wanted to. Everybody here thinks I'm a helpless female who can't carry a log from the porch to the fire. How do women exist in this world?"

"Use it to your benefit. Lie low and observe. And be careful, Ms. Kidd. There's more than one reason why they might want to keep you from getting too close."

It was with this last word of caution that I

disconnected and rounded up Nick. He wasn't entirely thrilled about the idea of leaving his dad behind, but after a short argument in hushed tones intended to hide phrases like "you can't tell me what to do" and "you're as reckless as she is," they went their separate ways. (I didn't think too much about the "she" in that latter statement.)

Nick pulled onto the dirt road. At home, he still drove the same Toyota pickup truck he'd had when we first met, which made him more qualified to drive Tully's vehicle than I was. I considered the acceptance of my idea by Kathy and Tully a small victory and hadn't made an issue out of how Tully had given driving permission to Nick and not me.

So yes, I told Nick I had a plan, but no, I did not tell him the details. I didn't want to worry him by the fact that I'd used the Batphone to call Loncar or that we were about to cozy up to the proprietor of a cowboy bar in an unfamiliar town. Nick had married me. Surely he knew I had a plan. Most definitely he knew not to ask for details.

The access road that led to the ranch was about half a mile long, and we traveled that distance in the comfortable silence that developed between married people who placed complete trust and respect in each other. Nick waited until two cars passed and then pulled onto the main road.

"I don't trust you," he said.

"How can you possibly not trust me after all this time?"

"I trust you in *life*. I just don't trust you right now.

There's no way you believe you're going to find a replacement act for the weekend in a town you've never been to before."

"You're right about that. Barring any musical miracles, I don't see us stumbling onto a band looking for a pop-up gig." I held my hand up in front of me and inspected my nails, as if I had no concerns in the world. Clawing Joey's nail out of the dirt of the arena had left my fingernails in a particularly sorry state. Maybe I could schedule in a manicure while we were out.

"Are you going to share your plan with me, or am I just to be your driver on this trip?"

I gazed out the window at the passing field of corn and made a decision. I might not want to share the details of my conversation with Loncar, but Nick was my ride-or-die, and in my world, that meant confiding in him about clues I'd discovered.

"I need a little leeway to make it happen, but once I get the ball rolling, I'll clue you in."

"So, then where are we going?"

"Let's start with the sheriff's office." I reached into my pocket and pulled out the bandana and nail, which I held up for Nick to see. "I found this in the arena after Lulu's accident."

"That looks like Joey's lucky nail."

"His 'lucky nail'? Did he tell you something about it?"

"He said it was from the horse his great-great-grandfather rode when they first settled the ranch. It's been passed down from generation to generation. Joey had it dipped in eighteen-karat gold to preserve it and kept it with him as a talisman."

"When did he tell you that?"

"Last night after our ride. It probably fell out of his jeans then."

"It couldn't have. He had it at the dinner table. Remember? When he was giving me a hard time about not being dressed for dinner—and don't get me started on that—he kept tapping it on the table."

"You're right. Then how'd it get to here?"

"I've got a couple theories about that. Joey was found dead in the stables. One, if this nail fell out of his pocket during some sort of scuffle, then it could have accidentally gotten stuck in the shoe of Lulu's horse and fell loose when they were riding."

"Possible, but unlikely," Nick said. "Lulu and Billy had been on a ride together before she entered the arena."

"That makes it seem like the nail was already in the dirt. Maybe whoever killed Joey took it as a souvenir and dropped it?"

"That makes the murder sound premeditated."

"We don't know that it wasn't." I picked up the nail and held it in front of me, turning it from side to side until I identified the inscription. "If someone intended to kill Joey, waiting until we arrived was a good way to double the suspect pool."

"Yes, but what would be our motive? We came to check out the ranch as a possible investment. Joey was the one who listed the ranch for sale. It's a lot better for my dad if Joey's alive than if he's dead."

"That's what I thought," I said.

Nick turned from the main road onto a narrow two-lane street. Colorful storefronts lined it. A store called Cowboy Collectibles sat between two clothing shops. One had an end-of-season-sale sign in the window, and the other had a chalkboard tent sign advertising new merchandise. I checked my phone's GPS and pointed down the street. Nick misjudged a speed bump, and the truck bounced over it, scraping something on the street and jostling my bones.

"Park here," I said suddenly.

Nick parallel parked the truck in a vacant space. "Seems the likeliest suspect would be someone who doesn't want the ranch to sell," he said.

"Why, Nick Taylor, I do declare I've rubbed off on you."

I unclipped my seat belt and turned toward him. His cowboy hat sat on the seat between us, and he picked it up. I put my hand on his arm and stopped him. He was on the dirty side for a cosmopolitan shoe designer, but as a ranch hand, he was starting to look the part. His curly hair, matted to his head from his hat earlier, had dried and curled back up, wilder and more free than how it appeared when he tamed it with gel in his professional life. A day of exposure to the sun had tanned his face, but his sunglasses left a white stripe by his temple. His laugh lines, crinkles by the outside of each of his eyes, were marked by the sun too. I had always been able to tell when Nick was joking or serious based on those crinkles, but now, they were part of his resting expression. My pulse quickened, and I understood the popularity of cowboy rom-coms.

Maybe instead of Zane Grey, I should have packed one of those books with a cover featuring a bare-chested man.

"Why are you looking at me like that?" Nick asked.

"Like what?"

"Like you're hungry and I'm dinner."

"Remember how you responded that time I wore leopard print to blend in with the mob wives?"

I knew the moment Nick figured out what I meant. Color blossomed on his cheeks. A group of teens on the street outside cut in front of our parked truck, and he held up his hat to shield us while he leaned across the seat to kiss me.

"You didn't happen to pack anything leopard print, did you?" he asked in a husky voice. "I can turn this truck around and head back right now if you want."

"Not before we conduct our business." I leaned forward and planted a kiss on his lips. "But if you want to stop at one of those boutiques on the way back, I'll see what they have in the way of animal-print underwear."

"You're killing me, Kidd."

I opened the truck door. We were among less than a handful of people on the sidewalks. A couple window-shopped in front of us, pausing to take in the various displays along the way, and a stooped rodeo clown dressed in mismatched patterns and prints sat on a bench across the street in a public park. I met Nick around the front of our truck and grabbed his hand. He was the one constant in a sea of weirdness. My lifeline.

We entered Cowboy Collectibles, and a cowbell mounted to the door announced our presence to the purveyor.

"Howdy," said an older man from behind a row of glass counters. He had a fringe of white hair and neatly trimmed white facial hair. His glasses had magnifiers attached to the lenses, and he peered at us over the tops of his frames. He was dressed like Cody and Angus, in a cowboy hat, plaid flannel shirt, and jeans held up by a belt with a gold buckle. It blew my mind how nobody around here acted like their wardrobe choices were ironic.

"Nice day to be out," the man said. "You folks new to the area?"

"Day-trippers," I answered before Nick could reply. "We're on our way to Atlantic City, but we stopped in town for dinner."

"Most folks would get dinner in Atlantic City," the man said. "'Course most folks wouldn't come into a collectible store if they wanted something to eat either." He took off his glasses and laid them on the counter next to a silver polishing cloth and a mat loaded with bright objects. "Don't matter much to me why you came into my shop instead of one of them touristy traps that popped up on the street. Looking for something special?"

I glanced at Nick, and he nodded to me. We were at our best when we shared a joint mission, and knowing he supported my agenda gave me a boost of confidence. I pulled the bandana out of my pocket and unraveled it, revealing the gold nail I'd found in the arena.

"I found this on a nearby ranch," I said. "It was embedded in the dirt in the center of the arena. Can you tell me anything about it?"

The man reached out, and I handed him the gilded nail. He put his glasses back on and held the nail by the point, slowly turning it in front of him. He made "uh-huh" and "tsk" noises while he turned the nail over in his hands. Eventually, he looked up over the top of his frames and gestured for me to get closer.

"Found this in the arena, you said?" he asked.

I nodded.

"As far as a decorative item goes, it's not a bad design, but this nail wouldn't secure a shoe onto My Little Pony." He set the nail on his cleaning cloth and narrowed his eyes in suspicion. "This nail belonged to Joey Baldwin. You mind telling me the real reason you ended up with it?"

13

SURE THING, PUMPKIN

Nick and I both stepped closer to the counter. I stared at the nail on the velvet mat.

"Like I said, I found it," I said.

"On your way to Atlantic City?" he asked.

I glanced at Nick, not so much wanting his reassurance but his help in crafting a plausible cover story. He stepped up to the counter. "Truth is, we snuck away from the ranch so we could be alone. Atlantic City represents a measure of privacy between consenting adults, if you know what I mean."

I put my hands behind my back and slipped off my wedding ring then tucked it into my back pocket. The shop owner looked back and forth between Nick and me. Nick, having spent his day working outside, looked every bit the cowboy. He was tan and lean, and he smelled like dirt and sweat. I, on the other hand, looked like a woman who spent most of her day inside, curled up on a sofa with a copy of *Riders of the Purple Sage* recently purchased from the local bookstore. In our regular life, we looked like we belonged together. Here? We were a weekend fling.

I put my hands on the edge of the counter. I'd gotten some sun, too, and a white tan mark was left on my ring finger. The shop owner noticed it and nodded, as if this was the evidence he needed.

"Can't say it's the first time love bloomed between employees and guests on a ranch. Doesn't matter much to me how you live your lives. You seem like nice people, and nice people deserve to find each other, no matter what brings them together. Too bad you didn't meet under other circumstances." He pointed to the nail. "As for this, I recognize it. I'm the one who made it for Joey."

"It's... it's not from the 1800s?" I asked. Nick gently elbowed me. I glanced up at his face and back at the shop owner. "I mean, like I said, it looks old, and I just thought, maybe it's been there for... generations."

He smiled. "It's not a bad thing that Taylor Sheridan made everybody think about these ranches in terms of generations. Business has been up since *Yellowstone* came out, and I say if that man has an idea for a spin-off, Hollywood should give him the money to make it. But nails like this are a dime a dozen. Joey had an idea to have gold horseshoe nails made up to sell as keepsakes for the Down Home, but they never took off."

"So you made more than one of them?"

"I made three." He pointed at the nail. "That's

eighteen-karat gold. Not particularly durable, but it looks nice." He picked the nail up and smoothed out the bend with his fingers. "Problem with gold is that the higher the karat, the more pliable the metal. If he'd gone with ten-karat, I doubt I'd have been able to bend it like that, but it wouldn't have looked as special."

"Do you know what happened to the other two?"

"I'm guessing he gave one to his wife," he said. "The ladies tend to like things like this."

He directed this last observation at Nick. I was so tired of being treated like a nonentity because of my second X chromosome that I reached out and plucked the nail from his fingers to bring his attention back to me.

"If someone lost it, they're long gone." I glanced back up at Nick. This time, he wasn't concerned by me. He stared directly at the shop owner.

"Could you give me a moment of privacy, honey?"

Even though he never broke eye contact with the owner, I was pretty sure he was talking to me.

"Sure thing, pumpkin." I forced a smile at the shop owner and left the two of them by the counter. I still had the nail, but neither of them seemed to care. After one backward glance, I pulled the door open and left, with the cowbell announcing my exit.

While Nick conducted his own version of super sleuthing (or, possibly, bought me a keepsake for our trip), I sat on the bench out front and pulled out my phone. I'd left the ringer on silent, and there were two missed calls from Loncar. That was unusual enough for me to forget all about Nick and the nail and immediately call the detective back.

"Loncar," he answered.

"You sound uptight. What happened to hello? Or maybe you should saying howdy."

"Have you already talked to Maverick?"

"Nick and I got waylaid. We're heading there next, I think."

"Don't. I made a couple calls on your behalf."

"And?"

"Problem solved."

"You found me a band? Can I say *I* found them? I've got a credibility problem at the Down Home, and it would be awesome if I could do something for a change."

Loncar ignored me. "Be there to greet him. Yours is the name he'll have."

"Him? One guy? I volunteered to provide entertainment for the whole weekend. Kathy said they usually sell hundreds of tickets to these things. Are you sure your guy can handle that?"

Loncar, predictably, ignored that too.

"Okay, fine, I'll trust you. I have to, don't I? You know this world, and I don't. But if Yosemite Sam shows up with two turntables and a microphone, we're going to have a serious talk about your efficacy."

"You should clue your husband and his dad in to your plan so they play along, but you're going to need to sell it. As far as anybody there is concerned, you're the one who set this thing into motion."

I thanked Loncar, though I wasn't too confident about his solution.

Nick exited Cowboy Collectibles after I hung up. He held a large brown shopping bag. I stood from the bench. "What happened after I left?"

"I impressed upon the owner how important it was that he not tell anyone about our visit."

"How?"

"That's between gentlemen."

"You know, I'm getting tired of this macho bullsh—"

Nick pressed his finger to my lips and held out the bag. "For you."

I took the bag and carried it to a nearby bench. Inside was a large boot box. I glanced at Nick, and he smiled.

"Open it."

I pulled out the box and set it on the bench then lifted the lid and unfolded the tissue paper. Inside was a pair of red leather Lucchese cowboy boots. They had a snipped toe and tan stitching on the shaft. I pulled one out of the box and held it, feeling a bit foolish but also a little bit excited. I'm a sucker for new shoes, and just the smell of the leather was intoxicating.

"Ever since I saw *Footloose*, I've wanted to date a girl in red cowboy boots," Nick said, "so I can't say this gift is all about you."

I ran my fingers over the stitching. "This doesn't change anything. I'm not ready to be your little lady."

"You'll never be my *little* lady," he said, making a point of looking at my butt.

I swatted him. "That's not what I meant, and you know it."

"How about we get you properly outfitted for a week on a ranch?" Nick pointed at a clothing shop near us. "You might feel more like you fit in if you're not wearing borrowed clothes."

If anyone was waiting for us back at the ranch, they were going to have to wait some more. I wasn't going to kid myself that Kathy was standing by the door with bated breath for my return. No one had missed me thus far, and I doubted they missed me now. And the person I wanted to spend time with was the one who had just bought me shiny new red cowboy boots. Maybe Nick was right. Maybe I was the one keeping myself from fitting in.

Nick spent the next two hours in a chair outside a fitting room. I worked far harder than that, trying on and taking off a variety of western-cut shirts in floral, plaid, and bandana prints. The pile I amassed by the register would have made Beth Dutton from *Yellowstone* proud. I even added a leopard-print bra and panty set as a surprise for Nick for later. Before we left, I selected a couple postcards from a rack by the counter and a child-sized Stetson for Nick's half sister, Chiara, who had recently gone back to Italy. When we left, I was doubly thankful for Nick's presence since he volunteered to carry half my bags.

Street parking had filled up, and the likelihood of finding another space was slim. Nick unlocked the truck, and I put my packages in the back and then sat inside the truck and changed into my new boots. We locked up and strolled through town arm in arm. (The thing nobody tells you is that strolling arm in arm while wearing cowboy boots is not without challenges.) We crossed the street and sat on a park bench, enjoying the peace that comes from having no particular place to go.

"You miss her, don't you?" Nick asked. I glanced at his face. "The cowboy hat. It's for Chiara, right? She's going to love it."

Chiara was a six-year-old Italian girl who happened to share Nick's DNA from a bizarre set of circumstances that sounded like something from the Jerry Springer Show. She'd returned with Nick and his dad after a trip to Milan, and her striking similarity to Nick had left me with the kind of questions a wife doesn't particularly like to ask.

I learned the truth about Chiara last year, and while I lacked the maternal instincts most women were born with, young girls appeared to be the sweet spot in terms of me bonding with a child. Chiara and I didn't speak the same language, but we connected through the language of sparkly clothes.

The week after the awards banquet, Senior accompanied Chiara back to Italy. His gift to Nick and me was a month to ourselves while he stayed with Chiara's grandmother, a former footwear model he'd met back when he ran the company. It was a few years after Nick's mother had died, and a lifelong friendship had blossomed. Even Senior's French bulldog, Bardot, had made the trip with them, requiring a battery of tests and documentation to allow her to travel internationally. Senior may be seventy-five, but he was not without agency.

Despite the relaxing time we'd spent in town, Nick seemed troubled by something other than Joey's murder. I reached out and threaded my fingers through his.

"What's wrong?"

He didn't answer at first. I waited, having learned the best thing I could offer him was silence until he wanted to talk. The breeze kicked a crumpled piece of turquoise paper past the toe of my new boots, and I would have gotten up and tossed it into the nearby trash bin if I wasn't more focused on being there for Nick.

"I'm worried about him," he said. "This ranch thing was funny at first, but he's treating it like it's more than an investment. It's almost like he sees himself moving out here and living in the bunkhouse with Cody and Angus and helping to run the place."

"Is that so bad?"

"He's seventy-five years old and is recovering from a hip injury. When he went to Italy with Chiara, I thought he'd drop her off and then come home, but he stayed for over a month. Ever since he came back, he's been different."

"Different how?"

"Like he wants to get in one more big adventure before he—" Nick didn't finish his sentence, but I knew what he was thinking.

I squeezed his hand. "Your dad has always sought out adventure. This isn't a last hurrah; it's his next hurrah. And if it isn't the ranch, then it might be something else. He has a curious mind, and he passed that down to you. It's what allowed you to diversify into the sneaker business. It's what makes us compatible."

"For as long as I can remember, my dad was a sane, stable person. But lately, it's like he's off the rails. Buying a Maserati, going to Italy for a month, now looking to buy a ranch—it's like he's lost his mind." He paused for the briefest moment, but before I had a chance to say anything, he continued. "Honestly? He's starting to remind me of you."

14

THE PRIVILEGE OF BEING IN MY CONFIDENCE

NICK'S ATTEMPT TO LIGHTEN THE MOOD OF OUR conversation did not go unchecked, but I took the bullet in the name of love. Neither one of us knew what was behind Senior's sudden interest in owning a dude ranch, but for now, it seemed worthwhile to play along.

Now that we'd found out the history of the horseshoe nail and solved the problem of the weekend entertainment, I had less of a mission in town. Nick knew half of that, but he'd earned the privilege of being in my confidence.

"So," I said casually, "I spoke to Detective Loncar."

"When?"

"Before we left. I recognized that I'm out of my element at the ranch, and I thought maybe he could help us."

"From Ribbon? What help do you expect him to give you from two hours away?"

"Exactly the kind he did. He's the one who told me about the Boot Strap, but we don't need to go anymore."

"Why not?"

"He called me back while you were in the collectible store. He arranged our entertainment while we were talking to the guy about the nail."

"That's good, right?"

I shrugged. "I guess so. I was looking forward to talking to Maverick and doing something myself. *You* know I'm capable. So does Loncar. I'm used to having autonomy, but this whole trip is just me being told to sit down, relax, and let the adults handle the problems."

"To be fair, that's what people tell you back in Ribbon too. You just don't listen. Why are you listening now?"

"Your dad," I said. "This whole trip is for him. If he's honestly considering investing in a dude ranch, then he should be allowed to make the decision himself without my input, right? So I'm trying to just lie low and let things unfold. But then Joey went and got himself killed, and Lulu got thrown off her horse, and the musical act canceled—"

Nick turned me to face him. He put his hands on my shoulders and leaned down so we were looking into each other's eyes. "You didn't kill Joey, right?"

"You know that I didn't."

"And you didn't toss Lulu from her horse, right?"

"You know I didn't do that either."

"And the Yee-Haws. You didn't double-book them? Or

tell them to choose another gig over the one at the Down Home?"

"I know what you're trying to do, and I appreciate it, but it doesn't change how everybody at the ranch has been treating me. You went out on a daybreak patrol with Tully, but Chef won't even let me help clear the table. So far, my only friend is the cat."

"I thought you were friendly with Mysti."

"Before we left, Mysti started hanging crystals over each of the ranch entrances to ward off negative vibes."

Nick looked concerned.

"I think she wants to talk about manifesting tonight after dinner."

"How about we get dinner in town?" Nick said, feigning interest in the restaurant scene.

"Just don't relegate me to the sidelines, okay? I get antsy when I'm not on the field."

"Sure thing, Kidd." He put his arm around my neck, pinning it in the crook of his elbow, and kissed my forehead. "Now let's get back to the ranch so I can tell everybody how you solved their entertainment problem."

We walked back to the truck, but we weren't destined to leave just yet. Despite Nick's attempts to start the engine, it sputtered then stalled. It wasn't until he'd tried three times that he noticed the gauge that earlier had displayed a full tank of gas was pointing to empty.

"Didn't Tully say the truck was full of gas?" I asked.

"It was," Nick replied. "I was with him when he filled the tank."

"But it's on E, and we've only driven about six miles."

I hopped out of the truck and got onto my hands and knees to peer under the truck. (It was somewhat freeing to discover that I didn't give a whit about getting my heavy-duty ranch clothes soiled by crawling around on the ground.) A dark stain was on the ground below the tank, and a small river ran from the puddle to the storm drain by the curb. Nick's cowboy boots stepped down from the other side of the truck, and the driver's side door slammed shut. His boots stopped by the drain, and his fingers appeared, swiping across the surface.

A car drove past, too close for comfort, all things considered, and I pushed myself up to a standing position and looked at Nick on the other side of the truck. "The gas tank is leaking, right? That looks like a leak."

"It's a leak, all right," Nick said. "Grab the jack from the bed of the truck. I'd like to take a closer look. Unless you'd like to assert your independence and do it for me."

"We'll do it together."

Nick gave me a funny look, and I realized that, while I wanted to be treated like an equal, it didn't make a whole lot of sense for both of us to get on the dirty public street underneath the truck if we didn't have to.

It took us about twenty minutes to get the truck raised, and don't think I wasn't ready to crawl underneath it because I was. But it wasn't Nick who stopped me from doing my best *Some Kind of Wonderful* impersonation. It was the owner of another set of cowboy boots who strolled up, no doubt checking out what trouble we were dealing with, and when I pulled myself up by the bumper, I learned those boots belonged to Sheriff Parker.

"Mr. Taylor, Mrs. Taylor," the sheriff said with a touch to the brim of his hat. "You folks get a flat tire?"

"Wish it were that simple," Nick said. "Seems the truck's out of gas."

"There's a station about a mile away," the sheriff said, pointing down the road. "Follow me back to the station, and I'll loan you a gas can."

I put my hands on my hips. "That won't help much with a cut gas line."

"Come again?" the sheriff asked.

Now that I had his attention, I pointed at the gas tank. "When we left the Down Home, we had a full tank. Now we're empty, and there's gasoline under the truck."

"Gas would evaporate," the sheriff said. "Besides, this is a busy street. Would be hard to tamper with a gas tank without being spotted."

"Would it?" I asked. "Because somebody did. While we were shopping. How hard could it be? Maybe somebody had a... I'm just spitballing here, but maybe somebody put a knife on the end of a hockey stick and stuck it under the truck like so." I made a motion as if I were sawing the truck in half from the underneath side. You don't have to say it. Even I knew it was among my less plausible theories.

Sheriff Parker seemed to realize the last thing I wanted to hear was that I was wrong, though, so he kept the obvious response to my theory to himself, slightly improving his stock. "You're not going to drive it anywhere like it is, so let's get you towed to a mechanic."

"But—" I started to say but stopped when I saw Nick's face. He shook his head imperceptibly. For whatever reason, he didn't seem to want to talk while the sheriff was within earshot.

15

NO WOMEN IN THE BUNKHOUSE

TRUE TO HIS WORD, THE SHERIFF MADE A PHONE CALL, which resulted in the appearance of a tow truck and the absence of our way home. The second problem was solved by the sheriff again when he volunteered to cart us back to the Down Home. Considering our lack of other options, we accepted his offer and were on our way within the hour.

The sun was setting, and the sky was awash with shades of coral, lavender, and sienna. The storm clouds that had threatened to move in earlier kept on moving, leaving behind chilly, damp air but no signs of rain.

Most people who spent time around Nick and me recognized that we have a good relationship. We chatted easily, enjoyed many of the same interests, and were comfortable showing affection. But during the ride back to the Down Home, none of that was on display. Sheriff

Parker drove an SUV, and I offered to sit in the back seat on the ride. I left the conversational responsibilities to Nick and got lost in my thoughts.

Something about the events in town troubled me—and not just the gas situation. Volunteering to solve the entertainment problem had been just one of the many ways I'd tried to help out since we arrived at the ranch, but it was the first offer that hadn't been met with resistance. Kathy must have other possible solutions in her back pocket, and if not, then someone else at the ranch would. I'd met Kathy, Joey, Tully, Angus, Cody, and Chef—and Mysti, who might not be an employee but was part of the group by marriage. If they truly didn't have a network on which to rely, then there might be more problems with the ranch than anyone was letting on.

And why would the sellers of a ranch keep something like that to themselves? Depending on the severity of the problems, they might keep a prospective buyer from seeing the ranch as a sound investment. And *that* directly affected Nick's dad.

Sending Nick and me into town in a truck with a cut gas line had kept us away for longer than we'd intended. I'd gone from wanting to help out with the problems on the ranch to needing to keep Nick's dad safe, and being away from the ranch while trying to book entertainment for the weekend was the least effective way to do so. My anxiety level rose, and I silently urged the sheriff to drive faster. It had been foolish to listen to Senior when he said he wanted to stay behind with the others. He was a seventy-five-year-old man who had never quite recovered from a hip injury a few years back. He was practically helpless, and we'd left him to fend for himself in a hornet's nest.

By the time we turned off the main road and onto the dirt drive, I was convinced that someone at the ranch didn't want it to sell and that Joey's murder and Lulu's riding accident were related. Without the horseshoe nail clue, nobody else would have connected those events, but I had. I had the clue wrapped up in a bandana in my pocket. I also had information about the clue that didn't fit what I'd originally been told, which made my information muddy.

The right thing to do would be to turn the horseshoe nail over to Sheriff Parker and tell him how I'd found it. But first things first. I had to make sure Senior was okay.

The sheriff parked the SUV out front, and I was out of the back seat and on my way inside before he turned the engine off. I ran to the ranch entrance and entered, unsure what I would find.

What I found was an empty house.

"Hello?" I called out. My voice echoed around the interior, bouncing off the leather sofa and wooden fixtures.

The saloon doors to the kitchen swung open, and Chef came out. "Hey, Samantha. The rest of the crew already ate, but I've got brisket and cornbread with your names on it. Hey, Nick."

I turned around and saw Nick and the sheriff enter

the house. Sheriff Parker scanned the interior, taking in everything from Mysti's table to Chef to the roaring fire. "Chef," he said.

Chef said, "Hi, Sheriff. I didn't know you were joining us. Want me to fix you a plate?"

"Where is everybody?" I asked.

"In the bunkhouse." He directed his attention to Nick. "Your father suggested the boys get a poker game going. He's out there with Tully, Cody, Angus, and the band."

"The band?" I repeated.

"The singer," he said. "His band is coming later." His forehead creased, and a series of lines deepened across the surface. "You're the one who arranged for them to play, right?"

"Right," I said slowly. Maybe Loncar had called in a favor to Maverick from Ribbon. Maybe the club owner had come through for us after we left—or maybe the Blues Brothers had shown up to take the spot promised to the Good Ol' Boys.

"He said something about canceling a gig in the area so they could play here. I have to admit, I didn't know you were a fan of country music, but when I heard they play Willie, Waylon, and Cash, well, that's exactly what we like around here. You saved the day."

"I told everybody I could help," I said aloud, but the voice in my head said a few other choice words.

I'd talked to exactly one person about my need to find a replacement act for the ranch. And that one person was Loncar. Loncar and Senior were friends, and the fact that a former homicide detective was at work finding us an undercover alternative had a surprisingly calming effect on me. But an operation like this could easily blow up in our faces, and I thought it best to check on things, to make sure we were all on the same page.

"Have a seat," Chef said. "I'll bring out your food."

"None for me," I said. "I want to go to the bunkhouse."

"Kidd?" Nick asked. "You were starving an hour ago. Don't you want dinner?"

"I could use a plate," Sheriff Parker said. He swung his leg over the bench and sat down at the table. Nick hovered next to him, wanting to sit down and have dinner too.

"Won't take but a second to get the grub ready," Chef said. "I even made something special for you."

I relented and took the seat across from Nick. Chef brought out a platter of carved brisket and a bowl of creamy macaroni and cheese made with wagon wheel pasta. He winked at me and set the bowl in front of my plate. He went back into the kitchen and returned with coleslaw and fresh jalapeno cornbread then made another trip and returned with two mugs of cold beer. He set one in front of Nick and one in front of me.

"You staying long enough for a beer, Sheriff?"

"I'll take a sarsaparilla, if you've got it."

"Coming up."

I swear, if I didn't know any better, I'd say the sheriff was having some fun at my expense.

The next half hour was filled with the sounds of forks, knives, and spoons scraping plates and bowls. My hunger returned with a vengeance, and I sated it with more than I'd eaten in two days. Chef checked on us periodically, not clearing anything until we proclaimed we (I) were done and even then giving us (me) another ten minutes to change our (my) minds. Nick and Sheriff Parker had stopped after seconds. I'm a sucker for mac and cheese and went in for thirds.

The food had left me feeling lethargic and ready for a nap, but when Sheriff Parker asked Nick if he'd like to check out the poker game, I instantly became alert. "I'll come with."

"No women in the bunkhouse," Chef said. "Ranch rules."

"Stay here," Nick said before I could properly express my reaction. He kissed my forehead. "I'm going to go check on my dad."

I wanted to protest, to remind Chef and Nick and Sheriff Parker that it was the twenty-first century and maybe they should reexamine a couple of their ranch rules, but I kept quiet for the greater good. I went to my room for my Zane Grey book. I'd forgotten to close my door earlier, and the orange-and-white cat was curled up in the center of the quilt. As I stroked his head, I heard sounds coming from the neighboring room. The sounds a bed might make when two people are engaged in romantic activities behind closed doors.

Chef hadn't mentioned Lulu and Billy, but if she

wasn't welcome in the bunkhouse, it made sense that her husband would have stayed behind to keep her company. If she could participate in what it sounded like she was participating in, then she must be feeling better. I grabbed my book, scooped up the cat, set him in the hallway, and closed my door behind me then went back out front to the fire. I took my bookmark out of my book and settled in to read. The front door opened, and Billy entered.

Tonight, he wore a turquoise western shirt with yellow flower embroidery. His boots were turquoise leather. He might be on my person-of-interest list, but I still admired his willingness to coordinate.

"Hey, Sam." He sat down in the nearby club chair and hung his hands down on either side. "Don't let me interrupt your reading. I've been in the hospital waiting room all day, and I'm whipped."

I stuck my finger in the book to hold my spot and stared at Billy. The flickering light from the flame danced across his features, playing off dark circles under his eyes. "Lulu isn't here?" I asked.

"No. The doctors said she suffered a slight concussion. They said she'll recover, but Kathy insisted they keep her overnight for observation."

"Did Kathy go to the hospital with you?" I asked.

"No," Kathy said from behind me. "I stayed here to oversee the ranch."

I turned around and saw her come out of the hallway where I'd been a moment ago. The same hallway that led to Billy and Lulu's room, which I thought had been occupied.

But if Billy was with me and Lulu was at the hospital in town, then who had Kathy been entertaining behind closed doors?

16

GENERATIONAL BUSINESSES

KATHY'S PRESENCE IN THE HALLWAY THAT LED TO THE guest suites temporarily distracted me. She was the last person I had expected to see, especially in light of the sounds I'd just heard. I tucked my bookmark back into my book and kept my attention focused on the hallway behind her to see who might follow her out. My interest in the hallway probably lingered a little too long because when I shifted my attention back to Kathy, she was watching me with her own brand of suspicion.

I'd known Kathy for less than a day, so I didn't have a lot to judge her on, but there was one undeniable fact that transcended anything I might have picked up if I'd been at the Down Home for more than forty-eight hours. The wife of the recently deceased owner should have been grieving.

She wasn't.

From the day Senior first told us about this trip, he talked up Joey, the man who had listed the property for sale. You might have thought they were old friends the way Senior responded to Joey—a fact I'd wondered about until the day we arrived. Joey had a natural ease about him around the men, which created a welcoming—if disproportionately masculine—energy. Kathy had been on the sidelines all along, almost more like an assistant than an equal. Whose idea had it been to sell? And why? If she and her husband were on the cusp of their happily ever after, then shouldn't she be more broken up about his murder? Her lack of emotions was suspicious, to say the least.

"You and your husband were gone a long time," she said.

The cat rubbed his side up against her ankles, and she bent down to stroke him. He trotted through the dining area and into the kitchen. She poured herself a glass of whiskey from a sideboard and leaned against the support beam in the center of the room. She looked tired, with purple circles under her sunken eyes, made to look even more pronounced by the shadow cast by her cowboy hat. She looked at me with her own brand of suspicion as she sipped her whiskey, almost as if we were engaged in small talk and not a line of questioning.

"We ran into some trouble," I said. "Or, more accurately, some trouble ran into us."

"You were in an accident too?" Billy asked.

"No," I said quickly. "Not an accident. Tully's truck ran out of gas." I purposely didn't add the rest of the details, that we'd tracked down the origin of Joey's golden nail or that the tank had gone from full to empty while we were parked. I also didn't mention that we'd hitched a return ride from Sheriff Parker. Somebody around here knew something, and I wanted them to tip their hand. I could play poker too.

"I still say this place is jinxed," Billy said. "Only a fool would buy it after this weekend." He planted his hands on the arms of the chair and pushed himself to a standing position. "It's been a long day, and I'm not feeling particularly social. See you both in the morning." He stepped around the seating area and left Kathy and me alone in the main room.

I picked my book back up and opened to my page then scanned the words until I located my spot. At the one-sentence-per-day rate I was reading, I'd finish this book sometime next year. Kathy joined me by the fire, sitting in the chair Billy had vacated. So much for reading.

"The boys told me you found us a musical act for tomorrow night," she said. "Thank you. It's been one thing after another around here, and with Joey gone, I can barely keep my head above water."

"My offer to pitch in was sincere," I said. "You and your staff have been treating me like I can't do anything, but I can. I was invited here to help Nick's dad determine whether or not the ranch is a sound investment. The way I see it, you're either trying to treat me like a paying guest to show us the full experience or you're afraid I'm going to find out something to make him walk away from the deal."

Kathy sighed. She leaned back against the leather and kicked her feet out in front of her. The light from the fire flickered over her red cowboy boots, illuminating the buffed and conditioned leather.

I might not know a lot about life on a ranch, but I knew a lot about shoes. I'd spent years as the senior buyer of ladies' shoes for what the ranch hands might call a *highfalutin* store in New York City. It was where I'd met Nick (and his dad, funnily enough, but that was a story for another time), where I first experienced career success, and where I ultimately decided that there was more to life than the nine to five (some days more like nine to nine. Ahem.)

Kathy's boots weren't new, which didn't surprise me. They were red, broken in, and decorated with elaborate ivory stitching. With her foot resting on its heel and her other foot crossed over it at her ankles, I was able to see the soles. Even though the boot uppers looked to be in very good condition, her soles were in need of repair. Her right foot had a hole underneath the ball of her foot, and layers of insole peeked through. There's no way she would have worn those boots outside to do ranch business. The whole purpose of the boots as day-to-day footwear was their durability. I tucked the thought away to examine at a later time.

My observation of Kathy's boots wasn't as covert as I might have liked. She bent her knee and pulled off one boot and then the other, setting them neatly next to her chair. "My inside boots," she said. "They're my favorite pair, but they need to be resoled. I shouldn't wear them at all until I can take them to a cobbler."

"Nick's dad was a cobbler before he opened the shoe business," I offered. "In a different life, he could have soled your shoes."

"Generational businesses," she said idly. She shook her glass of whiskey, and the ice settled in. She held the glass up against the fire, downed the rest of the contents, and set the glass on the wooden side table, not concerned about condensation rings or the need for a coaster. I guess there was more than one reason it was called the Wild West.

"This ranch has been in Joey's family for generations," Kathy continued. "When we first met, the idea of a ranch as a business was a lark. I mean, I was a classic Jersey girl. I had the nails, the hair, the works. But I was in love, so when Joey proposed, I said yes. His father had a stroke within the year, and the ranch became Joey's responsibility."

"Where was Joey's mother?"

"His parents divorced when he was a kid. His father never remarried." She picked up her glass and stared at the contents, reduced to melted ice cubes and watered-down whiskey. The promise of it didn't seem to pass muster, so she set the glass back down. "We'd been married for less than a year. I went from being an advertising executive to interviewing cowboys and approving livestock purchases. I never thought this would be my life."

"Whose idea was it to list the ranch for sale?"

"When we didn't have any children, it was inevitable that the ranch would either leave the family or become defunct. Joey ignored that reality for a long time. But as we got older, the desire to travel got stronger. There's no closing the doors and taking two weeks off when you're a ranch owner, not if you're actively running the place. Every penny we have is tied up in the day-to-day."

"That doesn't sound like a good investment for Nick's dad."

"If he wants to run it as a cattle ranch, I agree. But over the past five years, I've been shifting our goal from raising cattle to hosting a western experience. You haven't gone out with the men yet, but those early-morning rides are glorious—the sun cresting over the horizon, the wind on your face while you ride, the feeling of a horse's strength and power under your body. There's not much like it."

"What happened to the cattle?"

"We sold them off at auction."

"And your horses?"

"We sold them, too, except for the ones in the stables. The care and maintenance of the horses will be a vital part of the ranch if it's going to be a tourist experience, but Tully's the best there is."

"He doesn't see the value in retirement?"

"Tully? He's a lifer. Freedom for him comes the moment he sits in that saddle."

Whether Kathy wanted to chat or experience quiet time by the fire became a moot point. A general ruckus sounded outside of the building, voices mingling with the sound of boots clomping on the porch. The door swung open, and Angus and another cowboy entered. I did a double take when I realized one of them was Senior.

Angus put his hands on Senior's shoulders and announced, "Looks like we've got ourselves a card sharp in our midst. Even the band lost money."

Senior's face was flushed with success. He patted his bulging shirt pocket and grinned at Angus and Sheriff Parker. "Don't underestimate your new boss, fellas," he said. "And don't feel too bad about giving an old man your lunch money."

"Where is everybody else?" I asked. From my quick cowboy inventory, we were missing a couple people.

"Your husband is outside with the singer," Angus said. "Don't worry, missus, he must have known better than to bet against his dad."

"And Cody?" I felt Kathy's stare on me, but I didn't acknowledge her. "Wasn't he out there with you?"

"He joined the game late," Angus said. "Got tied up with some chores in here after dinner. Last one in cleans up, but doesn't seem right to make him handle it when he played one hand. See you folks in the morning."

As Angus left, I shifted my attention from him to Kathy. But while I'd felt her watching me when I asked about Cody's whereabouts, I now caught her staring into the fire. Her face was pale despite the flame reflecting back against her skin.

"Turning in sounds like a good idea." She stood and picked up her glass then headed into the kitchen. I heard the back door close. I waited for her to return from the kitchen, say good night, and head into the hallway that led to her quarters. When she didn't reappear, I went into the kitchen to check on her.

The bowls of snacks from earlier were lined up on the counter, each covered in plastic wrap that secured them from random passersby who would have grazed on the contents indefinitely (me). The other kitchen surfaces had been cleaned thoroughly, and a rag hung over the faucet. I felt the corner of the rag for dampness, but it was dry. Whoever had cleaned the kitchen had not done so recently.

If I hadn't seen Kathy come into the kitchen, I might not have believed it. There were no signs of a person having come through here—no back door banging against the frame, no improperly closed refrigerator, no running tap water or carrots on the cutting table. I stood by the island and turned in a circle, trying to find something to convince me I hadn't lost my mind. At the far end of the kitchen, I noticed a pantry door. I approached it and pulled the door open, a little surprised to discover it wasn't a pantry at all.

I stared into the hallway. Straight ahead at the end of the hall was the door behind which I'd heard the creaking bed. On the right side of the hallway was the room where Nick and I slept, and on the left was Senior's quarters. The private living space for Kathy and Joey was upstairs, a part of the main house I had not yet seen.

I stepped back and held the pantry door closed while turning around then turned back. It seemed a person who had knowledge of the layout would be able to go from the bedrooms to the kitchen and out the back door without anybody out front seeing them.

It should haven't seemed like important information. This main house was huge, offering sleeping quarters for the owners and enough guests to make the running of the ranch profitable. I took a quick tally of who I already knew slept under this roof—Kathy, Lulu and Billy, Senior, Nick and me. That was four rooms. Did Chef live here? He certainly seemed to be here 24/7, but did that mean Mysti lived here too? Were there quarters for the bands who entertained on the weekends, or did they stay in the bunkhouse with Angus and Cody?

I'd already been told that Tully lived in a cabin near the stables, and the sheer proximity of that to the crime scene had given him opportunity to commit the murder. Tonight, I'd learned about the bunkhouse, and presumably that would put both Cody and Angus under the same halo of suspicion. Chef had admitted to being out to collect eggs early the morning Joey had been murdered, and the back door to the kitchen gave him easy coming-and-going privileges. Now it seemed as though anyone who resided in the hallway could have accessed the kitchen using the fake pantry door, thus sneaking out the back exit unnoticed. My suspect pool should have been shrinking, but this discovery made it expand.

As I stood by the pantry, the back door to the house opened. A burst of adrenaline shot through my chest, and I darted through the fake pantry and into the hallway. Nick stood at the opposite end, with his hand on the doorknob to our room. He seemed surprised by my sudden appearance through a door that, until I'd burst through it, looked like part of the wall. I held my finger up to my lips to keep him from saying anything. I crept through the hallway to meet him halfway.

"Where's your dad?" I asked in a whisper.

"He just went to bed. Why?"

"There's someone in the kitchen. They came in from out back. Wait here. I'm going to go around the front."

"Kidd—"

I held up my hand. "I'm not going to do anything. I just want to see who it is."

I couldn't predict if Nick was going to keep watch in the hallway, but if I was fast enough, I could catch the kitchen bandit myself. I left the hallway and entered the main room. It appeared to be empty.

Under the guise of retrieving my book, I strode into

the room, not bothering to mask the sound of my boots on the wooden floor. In fact, I purposely stepped off the worn carpeting to let my footfalls announce me. But I'd been right the first time. There was no one else there.

I tucked my book under my arm, went to the kitchen, and found the one person I never, ever, *ever* could have predicted I'd find.

17

COWBOY PATRIARCHY

By the expression on Detective Loncar's face, he was as surprised to find me in the kitchen as I was him. To his credit, he recovered first. He peeled back the plastic wrap over the bowl of potato chips and pulled out a handful.

"What are you doing here?" I asked.

"Nobody told you?" He bit into a chip and crunched noisily. "That's funny."

The pantry door opened, and Nick joined us. "Cat's out of the bag," he said to Loncar.

"You knew?" I asked Nick.

"Loncar was at the poker game," Nick said.

"How would I know that? No girls allowed in the bunkhouse."

Loncar laughed. "I didn't know that rule still stood."

"Freaking cowboy patriarchy," I muttered under my breath. "Is one of you going to tell me what's going on?"

Nick looked at Loncar, who nodded. "I've got this one."

Nick kissed my forehead. "I'm going back to bed." He paused. "I know you're going to want to talk about this when you come to our room. I've been up since four thirty. If I'm already asleep, all I ask is that you try to hold your thoughts until sunrise."

"Maybe I don't want to talk about any of this," I said, waving my hands around. "Did you ever consider that?"

"No," they said in unison. Nick laughed and left.

"City folk can't handle ranch hours," Loncar said after Nick was out of sight.

I turned back to Loncar. "You're as city as Nick."

It was then that I took in Loncar's appearance. I'd been savvy enough to borrow his jeans, but it never occurred to me that Loncar's day-off style was western all the way. His shirt was a navy-blue bandana print with pearl button snaps over a white undershirt. His jeans were faded to a midrange, broken in, and whiskered around his crotch and knee areas. His boots were amber suede, dusty and creased, devoid of fancy stitching like those Billy wore. He had a bandana jutting out of his back pocket, and a thick leather belt with a tarnished buckle held up his jeans.

He hadn't shaved for a few days, but instead of an unkempt scruff, his beard, mustache, and sideburns shadows looked neatly trimmed. A black cowboy hat sat on the counter behind him, and he picked it up and put it on.

I'd once had the opportunity to make over Loncar with the help of Senior, so I knew that underneath his formerly unfashionable exterior, he had potential for a man in his late sixties. After his divorce, he and Senior became friends, and Loncar somehow got game. I'd been blindsided by my reaction to Nick in cowboy clothes, and it troubled me not just a little bit that I had the same reaction to Loncar. Robin doesn't suddenly develop a crush on Batman! (Maybe that was a bad example?) This would not do at *all*.

If Loncar noticed my response to him, he kept it to himself. He pushed the potato chip bowl toward me, and I shook my head. I was too troubled about my unexpected attraction to Loncar to think about snacks.

Loncar covered the bowl with the plastic wrap and slid it back into the row of other bowls. He brushed his hands against each other over the sink, freeing his fingers from errant potato chip crumbs.

"It wouldn't be the worst thing in the world for us to get our stories straight," he said. "Is there a place we can talk?"

"Follow me."

I led Loncar out of the kitchen, through the great room, and out the front door. For all of the in-and-out traffic I'd seen since first arriving at the ranch, it struck me that this was an early-morning crowd and that the best time to get away with something covert was after everyone had gone to bed.

I rounded the side of the building and sat on a bench

that faced the stables. Loncar sat next to me. The friendly orange cat was off conducting important after-dark feline business, so for now, it was just the two of us.

"You never answered my question," I said. "What are you doing here?"

Loncar repositioned his hat on his head. "You asked me to help you find entertainment. I made a few calls, but no luck. It's not easy to find a band at the last minute, especially for a one-time gig."

"What do you mean?"

"The Down Home is for sale," he said. "Everybody in the business knows it. If this place were still going strong, it might be worth it to a new band. Get your foot in the door, help them out when they're in a pinch, and score a spot on their regular schedule. Not a bad thing to become known as the house band at a place like this."

"But that's not the case here," I surmised.

"Right. Trouble's been brewing for a while now. Infighting with management and now, a murder. Until new management decides what they're doing with the place, everybody's in a holding pattern."

"Buzzing around like a committee of vultures?"

"They're a committee when they're resting. Otherwise, they're a kettle."

"A kettle of vultures. Sounds as unappetizing as a kettle of popcorn made with sugar."

Loncar shook his head. "If this place closes, some people are going to win and others will lose. It's the way of the world."

"What do you mean?"

"This place has enjoyed a solid reputation for a long time. There are other ranches in New Jersey, but the Down Home has been around since the 1800s. With the surging interest in all things western, it's on an upswing. Joey's timing on selling the place is either curious or opportunistic."

"From what I've seen, nobody besides Senior is interested in buying it."

"You sure about that?"

"What are you getting at?"

"Seems like a murder might be a way to flip the picture and make it a buyer's market. Tell me about everything that happened since your party arrived."

"Are we just going to sit here asking each other questions?"

Loncar didn't respond to that one. He watched me for a few seconds, waiting for me to overshare in terms of intel. He knew me well.

I sighed. "About an hour after we got here, two other guests arrived. Billy and Lulu Cassidy. There's a cat around here somewhere, and he ran in front of the car, and Lulu smashed her car into that telephone pole." I pointed out front to the pole in question.

Loncar's forehead wrinkled. "She couldn't have been going too fast if she'd just arrived. You can't miss the main house, and an arriving guest would slow down to park."

"Right. But the dirt road was muddy, so when she hit the brakes, the car skidded. Her husband criticized her driving, and she said if he hadn't been drinking at dinner, she never would have been behind the wheel."

"Either of them sustain injuries?"

"Not from the accident," I said. "But Lulu was in a jumping accident this morning."

"I thought she was a guest of the ranch."

"She is. They both are. And they're more city slicker than me and Nick."

"City slickers don't get close enough to jumping rigs to have accidents," he said. "Did anybody see this fall?"

"Everybody saw the fall."

"You too?"

"Yes. I was"—I pointed to the far end of the field— "over there. With Mysti. She's Chef's wife. She's the only person around here who doesn't treat me like I'm helpless. We went for a walk after lunch."

"Where was everybody else?"

"Cody, Senior, and Nick were watching Henna and Tully from the side of the arena. Billy and Lulu joined them."

"I'm going to need more than names."

"Henna is a barrel racer, and she's Tully's niece. She lives nearby and uses the arena here to train. She's petite, has bright-red hair, and seems like she can handle herself around a group of rough cowboys. Mysti said Henna's been riding horses since she was a kid."

"Mysti's the blonde?"

"Yes. She runs a spiritual business in town called Mystical Treasures. She set up a table inside where she's going to sell crystals. I think you left your guitar propped up against it."

Loncar nodded, following easily. "I met Tully at the poker game. He's the ranch manager, right?"

"Yes. He lives in a cottage on the other side of the stable. Mysti said she can't imagine the Down Home without him. Everybody seems to have great respect for him, but I probably know him the least of anybody here. He kicked me out of the stables the morning after I found Joey's body. It was like he suspected me of spooking the horses."

"You didn't?"

"The horses were already spooked. My presence probably didn't help, but neither did Joey's murder."

Loncar leaned back against the side of the building. He kicked his feet out in front of him and looked at the deep purple-blue night sky dotted with hundreds of stars. I shifted my attention from Loncar to the sky and, for the first time since we'd arrived, stopped to take in the beauty of the surrounding land. The light came from the moon, and it was full enough to make visible the tree line, the fence, and a family of deer that grazed about a hundred feet away. I pointed to the deer, Loncar nodded, and we sat there, allowing our murder-case recap to lapse into silence while we admired the beauty of the great outdoors.

After a minute or so, one of the deer turned and fled. The others followed. I watched their silhouettes disappear into the darkness, and moments later, there was no sign that they'd been there.

Loncar picked up the conversation as if there hadn't been a break while we communed with nature. "Who else?"

"What?" (I was not so quick to transition.)

"Who else was at the arena when Lulu had her accident?"

"Cody. You met him at the poker game, right?" Loncar nodded. "Billy, Lulu's husband. Nick and Senior."

"Where was Kathy?"

"In town."

"Doing what?"

"Conducting ranch business. I don't know exactly what that entails, but after Lulu's accident, Henna rode into town to get her. I can't tell you much of what happened after that because I volunteered Nick's and my services to find a replacement act for the weekend."

"That's when you called me."

"Yes."

"It's not like you to ask for help. What exactly did you think I was going to do from Ribbon?"

"I don't know." I turned my face so the cool night air blew my hair back. It felt refreshing. I filled my lungs and felt them expand with the fresh air. Every breath I took out here felt like a recharge, like eating a bowl of vegetables felt for my body. "Ever since we arrived, I've been treated like a child. I've offered to help with a variety of things, and every time, I'm told to just relax. You know how I am. Relaxing stresses me out. So when Kathy told me how important it was to secure entertainment, I jumped at the chance to solve her problem. That time, she agreed." The one thing I didn't add was that, by showing up, Loncar had helped me fulfill my role as problem solver. If me calling for help was out of character, him providing the help was too. It was just one more mystery to add to the ever-expanding heap.

18

WHAT HAPPENS ON THE RANCH
STAYS ON THE RANCH

"WHAT EXACTLY IS YOUR PLAN FOR SATURDAY NIGHT?" I asked Loncar. "When you're supposed to perform?"

"I'll cross that bridge when I get there."

"But they think you're part of a band. It's great that you showed up with equipment, but what's going to happen when someone points you toward a microphone and expects you to sing for your supper?"

"Maybe I'll surprise you." He reached up and lifted his cowboy hat then shifted it so it sat lower on his head. This whole cowboy energy seriously threw me off my game. If a hat, stubble, and western-cut shirts could make me see Loncar in a different light, then what else was possible? I'd discovered a world I never knew existed, and as much as the employees perpetrated their own brand of authenticity, it was as foreign to me as if it were a Hollywood set left intact from John Wayne's days.

Exhaustion settled into my bones, and I yawned. It

had been a long day, and even though I'd been granted sleep-in privileges this morning while the others went into town, I was ready for slumber. Loncar stood and held out his hand. I glanced at it but pushed myself out of the chair.

"Ms. Kidd, as far as anybody here knows, I'm the lead singer for the country band that stepped in to perform this weekend. I'm here because you already knew me well enough to ask if I'd help the ranch out in a pinch. I know we have a—what do you like to call it?—complicated relationship, but that means something very different to them than it does to you."

"How do you know I say that?"

"Does it matter?"

"Yes."

He hesitated for a moment then said, "Senior told me."

I can't trust Nick's dad with anything!

"If you don't treat me like we're somewhat familiar with each other," he said, "people are going to get suspicious."

I narrowed my eyes. "Define 'somewhat familiar.'"

He glanced at my legs. "You could let it slip that you're wearing my jeans."

"Why would that matter to anyone?"

"When's the last time you borrowed another man's clothes?"

I thought back for a moment. When what Loncar was

insinuating became clear, I felt my cheeks flush. "But they'll think—"

"Yep, they will, but only if we sell it. They'll draw their own conclusions based on how we interact."

"But I told them—"

"Ms. Kidd, when's the last time you believed what someone *told* you over what their *actions* told you?"

Loncar had a point. "What about boundaries? Do we need to establish some? Or will you just accept that anything I may say or do while we're here is just in support of your cover?"

"What happens on the ranch stays on the ranch." He cracked a smile.

"I need to tell Nick and his dad."

"They both know the truth about us, and they both know the real reason I'm here. Nobody's marriage is in jeopardy."

"Right. Sure. Okay. Yes." I thought things through. "How many pairs of jeans did you bring?"

"Two. Why?"

"I'll bring you this pair tonight," I said, pointing at my thigh. "Two different people have commented on the wear marks. That means they noticed my jeans. If you show up wearing them tomorrow, they'll put two and two together."

Loncar nodded as if this was an acceptable solution. He stood. I glanced up at him. He was relaxed, with his thumbs hooked into the front pockets of his jeans. He held out one hand and pulled me up. I dusted off the seat of my jeans, and we rounded the house and climbed the stairs to the porch. Loncar held the door open for me.

I turned back to him and asked, "Is there anything else I need to know?"

"The rest of my band is arriving on Saturday. We sing Willie, Waylon, and Cash."

Loncar hadn't just shown up with a guitar. He'd put some thought into this. It was equal parts humorous and sobering. He wouldn't even be here if he didn't think there was a greater risk of danger because of the murder. In fact...

"Does Sheriff Parker know?"

"Ms. Kidd, I'm not a cop anymore. I'm a private citizen who resides in Pennsylvania. Sheriff Parker has jurisdiction over this ranch. There's no reason for him to think I'm anything other than what I say I am unless you give him one."

"What's the name of your band?"

Loncar didn't answer. For all the details he'd thought through, this one appeared to elude him. It was the simplest question of any I'd asked about his cover, and for him to not have a reply at the ready was inexcusable. It didn't matter how much I might cozy up to him in front of the others. People in bands don't become speechless when asked the name of their group.

"You called for Backup, right? That's our name." He cracked another smile, amused by himself. It wasn't terrible.

Loncar waited by the fire while I went to my room

and slipped off his jeans. Soft, even snoring came from Nick's side of the bed, and I tried my best not to wake him. My black turtleneck sweater was long enough to cover my panties but not by much. I grabbed a quilt and wrapped it around my shoulders then carried Loncar's jeans out front to the common area and handed them over. We went our separate ways—Loncar to quarters down another hallway, and me back to my room. I changed into my nightgown and grabbed my overnight bag then snuck out of the room. The rest of the house was shrouded in darkness. I tiptoed to the bathroom then washed up and brushed my teeth. The truth was, after a day on the ranch, I needed a shower.

(Yes, I know I didn't do any actual ranchy things, but still, how often do I get to say something like that?)

My reflection reinforced that need. My hair had picked up dirt from the wind, and smudges had mixed with sweat and left my hairline grimy. The black smear just inside the collar of my shirt was a telltale trace of my mechanic impersonation in town. I checked the state of my fingernails again. They were clogged with debris. The last thing I would have thought I'd need on this getaway was an orange stick.

A sign on the back of the bathroom door requested that guests limit showers to five minutes. I threw the locks on the door and tried my best to oblige, but something about the rules of this place irritated me to a degree I hadn't anticipated, and I lathered, rinsed, and repeated with abandon.

Rebellion felt good.

After a shower three times longer than the sign suggested, I turned off the water and dried myself, put my nightgown back on, packed up my overnight kit, and crept back to my room. A thin glow of light shone from underneath the pantry door at the opposite end of the hallway. I didn't think too much about it until I was halfway into the bed.

Shoot. I had been the last person in the kitchen. I must have left the light on.

Nick rolled over and draped his arm across me. "Hey, Kidd," he mumbled.

I moved his arm and threw back the covers. "I have to go to the kitchen," I whispered. "Hold my spot."

He grunted, and his gentle snoring resumed.

I slipped out of our room and stealthily crept down the hallway. The shower had done the opposite of reinvigorating me, and as I moved toward the light source, I felt a little bit like an overcooked noodle. When I reached the pantry door, I realized no doorknobs were on the outside, and since the door swung open toward the hallway, there appeared to be no way to open it from where I was. I left the hallway and went back around to the dining room then entered the kitchen from that side. The bright light inside darn near blinded me and shocked my system back into awake mode. Instantly, I turned out the light, leaving my eyesight compromised.

I couldn't see a thing. I had nothing to help me get back to my room other than my hands feeling my way along the hallway wall. Which would be fine once I reached the hallway, but first, I had to get to the other side of the kitchen.

I headed in that direction with my hands out in front of me to feel for obstructions. I ran into something—a barstool, I think—and it tipped away from me. I reached out and grabbed one of the legs before the whole thing clattered to the ground but then grazed my hip on the corner of the center island and cursed under my breath. That was going to leave a bruise.

I flicked the light switch back on then scanned the room to see if there was a switch on the opposite wall. Not seeing one, I did my best to map out the layout of the kitchen so I could make it across the room without banging into anything else. I switched off the lights again and closed my eyes, this time counting to thirty while they adjusted to the darkness. I opened them and crept forward, avoiding painful contact with the fixtures. I was across the room and out the pantry door when I heard the clank of something fall to the floor behind me.

I froze. Had I knocked something over without knowing?

The door to my room opened, and Nick pushed his head out. "Kidd?" He looked as if he'd been woken from sleep. His curly hair was matted to one side, and his stubble had become more pronounced, shading the lower half of his face in a shadow. He blinked lazily, as if the effort of keeping his eyes open was almost too much. But because Nick is Nick, he asked, "Are you okay?"

"I don't know. I mean, yes, I'm okay, but I don't know —" I pointed behind me. "I think I knocked something over in the kitchen."

He yawned. "It's late. Whatever it is, it can wait until morning." He stepped back and held the door open. I left the kitchen behind me and joined him in bed.

I lasted seventeen minutes before I got back up to investigate the noise.

(Nick was already back asleep.)

This time, I took a small flashlight from the end table. It provided enough light to guide me back through the dining room and into the kitchen, where I identified the noisy culprit—an aluminum sauce pan on the floor between the center island and the back door.

I stood rooted to the floor with all my attention on that pot for longer than necessary, mostly because I didn't want to believe what its presence said. I hadn't been anywhere near the back door. The barstool that I'd almost knocked over was on the opposite side of the island.

Someone else had been in the kitchen while I was here.

And then, a second thought came on the heels of that one. Someone else was *still* in the kitchen. Right now. While I was in the kitchen too.

I flashed my light around in a panic. I was alone. No one had followed me into the hallway, but—

The back door was not properly closed.

When inside your own house, you knew to close the

door if it wasn't properly closed. You knew there might not be a *specific* threat of someone choosing your house to enter in the dead of night, but still, you understood the importance of removing that threat by engaging the lock as a best practice. You knew that the locking mechanism embedded in the door provided enough of a safety measure to grant you the eight hours of peace you needed to release your paranoia against the unknown and sleep until morning.

You knew all those things without actively reviewing them. They became second nature, as unconscious as turning off the water after you washed your face or closing the refrigerator door after you snuck an extra slice of cake. Common sense didn't even enter the picture.

That was why I went to the back door to close it properly and throw the lock. Because at that moment, what I wanted more than I wanted anything else was to release my paranoia and sleep until morning.

But when I approached the back door, I saw someone running away. Without thinking, I pushed the door open and stared out, barely making out the silhouette of the person who'd been in the kitchen with me moments before.

19

NOT THE COWBOY WAY

My heart thumped against my ribcage. It hadn't been my imagination. Someone *had* been here. Someone had been inside the kitchen seconds ago. Someone who didn't want to be caught.

I could think of a lot of reasons one of us might be in the kitchen after dark. Snacks, drinks, picking at leftovers or checking out the menu for tomorrow. A person in the kitchen after the rest of us went to bed should not have been suspicious.

But why would someone hide when I entered? Why not just say hey, Samantha, pull up a chair and help yourself to some Chex Mix?

I could think of a lot of reasons a person might have been there, but I could only think of one reason they wouldn't want their identity to be known.

They were guilty of something a lot bigger than raiding the fridge.

I aimed my penlight into the night. If I had seen who it was, I might have been able to figure out what they were doing in the kitchen and why. But whoever had been here was gone, disappeared into the darkness like the deer had earlier.

I stepped back and pulled the door closed and triple-checked the lock then shivered from a cool breeze on my shoulders. Despite the cool nighttime temperatures, the window above the sink was open. I switched off the lights and peered out the window. The bench where Loncar and I had sat discussing his reason for being here was directly below me. If someone wanted to listen in to our conversation, this would have been the best spot.

I'd considered the theory that Joey was killed by a transient, but a transient would have been in another state by now. A person with something to gain by Joey being out of the picture would stick around to see where the pieces fell.

———

The next morning, I woke to an empty bed. The curtains were drawn, and the room was still dark. I checked my clock. It was nine thirty.

Nine thirty? How was that even possible?

I threw back the covers and opened the curtains. A shock of sunlight assaulted me. I quickly dressed in an Eagles sweatshirt and a pair of Loncar's jeans and pulled on my new cowboy boots. I was eager to find

Nick or Loncar and tell them what had happened last night. In the cold light of day, it seemed hazy, like a dream or a scene I'd read about in one of my westerns where my subconscious had inserted me into the narrative. But the penlight sat on my end table where I'd left it, enough evidence that I hadn't imagined my late-night trip to the kitchen or my near miss with the figure in black.

I left my room. I didn't want to be alone in the house, but nobody knew that. Until I found someone to tell, nobody knew about last night.

Chef was sitting at the dining table. As soon as he saw me, he stood. "Hey, Samantha. I just made coffee. Want some crepes?"

"Sure. Where is everybody?"

"Out for a ride. Your husband said to let you sleep in."

"Did he say why?"

"I imagine it's because you didn't sleep well." He looked concerned. "This thing with Joey is enough to give anybody nightmares. I was happy to go home last night even if it did mean getting up an hour earlier this morning."

I sat at the table and poured myself a cup of hot, steaming coffee from a carafe then added a healthy dollop of half-and-half. Chef came out of the kitchen with a plate of fresh crepes topped with berry compote. He set the plate in front of me.

"Do you want anything else? Bacon? Sausage? Biscuit?"

"The crepes are fine," I said. "I don't have a huge appetite."

"Not sleeping and not eating. That's not the cowboy way."

"So far I haven't been much of a cowboy."

Until now, Chef had kept to his responsibilities, serving the group and clearing the table. But now, he lowered himself onto the bench opposite me and propped his arms on the table.

"About that," he started. "I owe you an apology."

I didn't say anything, both because I was curious about what he wanted to apologize for and because I had a mouthful of food.

"You haven't had much of a ranch experience since you've been here, have you?"

I swallowed. "I'm not much of a ranch hand."

"That's just the thing. Just because you're not out there on a horse doesn't mean you can't join in, especially since your father-in-law is looking at buying the place. You deserve to get the same behind-the-scenes treatment as them."

"What do you have in mind?"

"I thought you could help me plan the menu for the party tonight."

"I'm not much of a cook either," I confessed.

"Don't need to be. What would you want to eat if you were going to a cowboy-themed party?"

"That's not a fair question."

"Why not?"

"I'd probably put out Slim Jims and biscuits." I thought back to Sheriff Parker and added, "And bottles of sarsaparilla."

"Sheriff Parker was pulling your leg with that one," Chef said. "He normally asks for an IPA."

I swallowed another bite of my crepe. The berries were bright and fresh, exploding into a sweet fruit medley against my tongue. The crepe was thin and cooked to perfection. Two days ago, I would have predicted ranch breakfast to be steak and eggs, but even the food here had turned out to be a surprise.

"You're serious?" I asked. "About me helping you with the menu for tonight?"

"Wouldn't have asked if I wasn't. You're exactly the type of person who comes out on a Saturday night. This ranch is a novelty, and the people who come might book us for their own parties if they like what they see. Monday through Thursday is about regular ranch business, but on the weekends we blow it up and deliver the tourist experience. I'd like to hear what that would be for you."

"Cast-iron skillets of biscuits. Homemade gravy. Wagon wheel mac and cheese. Isn't there a thing called *cowboy caviar*?"

Chef grinned. "Finish your breakfast. I'll get my shopping lists."

————

BY THE TIME the rest of the group returned from morning patrol, Chef and I had planned out the menu for the party, and I'd given him a few suggestions for his regular weekly menus too. He seemed open to my insights, though I wondered if he was going to add hot dog shish kebabs and cornbread casserole after we left.

The arrival of the rest of my party came with a certain amount of disruptive noise. Raucous male laughter and boot soles striking against the floors replaced the silence. Someone switched on the sound system, and music filled the interior.

I watched the men interact. Senior was at the center of the group, slapping Angus on the back and shaking hands with Cody. He had a huge smile on his face—as big as the day he had bought his Maserati. A bond appeared to be forming between him and the ranch employees, and it pained me to think that one of them could be behind the murder of the former owner and what that would mean if Senior took his place.

I stood up and walked toward Nick. Cody intercepted me and hooked his elbow through mine, swinging me around in a half circle to the beat of the music. "Woo-hoo!" he said. "We're having ourselves a party tonight!" He released my arm and hooked his other arm through Angus's, completing another half circle.

The door opened again, and Kathy came in. She watched the merriment from a few feet away. Cody spotted her and hooked his elbow through hers next. She looked at him with an expression of protest. He swung her around. The others backed up and gave them space. Senior clapped with the beat, and Nick and Angus joined in. It looked for a moment as if Kathy were enjoying herself, but then suddenly, she shook off his grip on her arm.

"It's too soon." She turned away from the group and went up the stairs. A few seconds later, a door slammed shut.

The general merriment subsided, and the crowd dispersed. The cowboys made their way toward the table, and Senior stood behind it with Loncar. Nick left them behind and approached me.

"Hey there, sleepyhead." He took his cowboy hat off and leaned down to kiss me. "If you're not careful, you're going to sleep through everything."

I grabbed his wrist and dragged him out front. The orange-and-white cat was back, sprawled across a patch of sunlight on the porch. He lay with his back legs stuck out, one front paw tucked underneath him while he licked the other and swiped it over his head.

"You're the one who slept through something," I said in an urgent hiss. "Last night. Someone was in the kitchen."

"The kitchen isn't off-limits. Somebody probably wanted a late-night snack."

"No, it wasn't like that." I relayed the details of my late-night encounter to Nick. At first, his expression was one of amusement. I had a history of blowing up situations, seeing suspicious behavior where (maybe) there was none. But when I reached the part about the partially open window above where Loncar and I had spoken freely and the figure who left out the back door, Nick's expression turned serious.

"You didn't see who it was?"

I shook my head. "It was a figure in all black—including a black hat—running away from the house at night. I held my flashlight up, but it was a little penlight, and it didn't illuminate much more than the back steps."

"How long did you stand there?"

"A couple seconds. When I realized I'd lost track of the culprit, I went back inside and locked the door. I turned out the lights and came back to bed."

"The kitchen light was on all that time?"

"Yes. Why?" As soon as I asked the question, I realized exactly why Nick had asked and why that mattered. Maybe I hadn't been able to identify the person running away, but they would have easily been able to see me. I'd been backlit by the kitchen light. I might as well have held a beacon over my head.

20

LAUNDRY DAY

"THERE ARE TWO POSSIBILITIES," I SAID. "THE PERSON hiding in the kitchen was so worried about not being seen that he or she didn't stop running until they were around the other side of the bunkhouse." I chewed my lip and considered the other possibility. "Or the person hiding in the kitchen knows my identity."

"If it's the second, then you need to be careful."

"That's just the thing, though. I haven't had a chance to *not* be careful. We've been here for a couple days now, and I haven't even been on a horse yet. The most dangerous situation I've been in was with you in town when we ran out of gas."

"That was inconvenient but not dangerous."

"Right. But think about it. I found Joey's body. Everybody here knows that. But Lulu was the one who had a riding accident. All I've done so far is sit on the sofa and read."

"And find a body, discover a clue, track down information from a source in town, arrange for a man on the inside, and discover a person hiding in the kitchen."

I didn't hear most of what Nick said. "*Try* to read," I amended. "I don't think I've finished an entire chapter yet."

I glanced over each of my shoulders as if someone might be lurking about as we spoke. "Chef was particularly friendly to me this morning. He asked for help planning the menu for Saturday night."

"That sounds right up your alley. You don't think his request was sincere?"

"Think about it. The easiest time to treat someone differently is when you're paying attention to them. And if someone is threatened by what I might have seen, then they're going to pay attention to me. If it was Chef, he'd rather keep me in his sights than let me go off on my own."

Before Nick had a chance to agree or convince me I was paranoid, the front door opened, and Kathy poked her head out. "There you are," she said.

Nick put on his hat. "Yes, ma'am. What can I do for you?"

"Not you. I meant Samantha." She looked directly at me. "I was hoping you could help me out today."

"Um, sure." I glanced at Nick briefly then back at Kathy. "What were you thinking?"

"Follow me."

I glanced at Nick.

He nodded. "I'll see you later," he said.

I hadn't forgotten about Kathy's suspicious behavior behind closed doors yesterday, although I wasn't nearly as concerned about her behavior as the identity of the person she'd been misbehaving with. If I had to guess, I would say she and Angus were having a fling.

Or had she been with Cody?

Or Chef? Or Tully? Or Billy?

In the past, I'd been burned by my habit of jumping to conclusions. Maybe it was better not to guess. Maybe it was better to shadow the ranch owner to see what I could pick up while in her presence.

"It's laundry day," she said. "We used to have a service that picks up and drops off, but when we changed our schedule to every other week, they suspended that service. You went into town yesterday, so I was hoping you could help me out with dropping off the laundry today."

"Of course."

"And while you're there, can you circulate around town and talk up the party?"

"Aren't you going to be with me?"

"I was away for most of yesterday, and with Joey—" Kathy's voice cut off abruptly. She looked away from me, out toward the open grounds, and allowed the wind to blow her long golden hair away from her face like it had done to mine last night. Her skin was tan and freckled. Her lips were faintly glossed—likely she'd used a tinted balm, not bold lipstick or super shiny lip gloss. Her ears were pierced, but she wore no earrings. Everything about Kathy seemed to be natural. As I studied her profile, she turned back to me. "A lot of people are watching me to see if I can handle the ranch without my husband. Some of those people are probably hoping I fail."

"That doesn't seem to be the cowboy way," I said.

"It was one thing for Joey to list the ranch for sale. It's been in his family for generations, and that decision didn't come lightly. But now that he's gone, I'm a single woman connected to this place through marriage. A ranch sale attracts two kinds of attention—interested parties like your father-in-law and vultures looking for a bargain. I'd much rather sell to the first type and not the second."

"Have you had other interest?"

"It's in my best interests to tell you that I have," she said. "Pit buyers against each other and drive up the price." She sighed. "The truth is, there have been inquiries but no solid offers. The trouble we've had lately hasn't helped matters."

"Can I ask a somewhat-impertinent question?"

"Shoot."

"Is it wise to throw a party with live music and an extensive menu when your husband..." I let my voice trail off. Kathy wasn't acting like a woman who'd lost her husband two days ago. She wasn't acting like a woman in mourning or a woman who was at a loss now that her better half was gone. I'd had the same observation yesterday when I first heard she'd gone into town, but saying so to her face put me in an uncomfortable spot and left me feeling cold and heartless.

After a long pause, Kathy said, "Joey and I were in the middle of divorce proceedings." Her voice was even. "It wasn't a secret on the ranch, but we tried to keep it quiet around town. The Down Home is a tourist destination. It behooves us to put on a friendly face and maintain a welcome environment. If word got out that we were anything other than what we seemed, people would stay away."

"You wanted your freedom back," I said. As soon as the words were out of my mouth, Kathy's behavior made sense. "You said you never wanted this life, that Joey took over the ranch when his father died unexpectedly and you were forced to give up the life you knew."

"Right. I gave it all I had, but it wasn't enough. Joey and I, we grew apart. The ranch was a convenient distraction for a long time, but when you watch your life tick away day by day, eventually you start to think you owe it to yourself to live the life *you* want, not lay yours down at the feet of someone else."

There wasn't much I could say in opposition to that. Years ago, I changed up my life for similar reasons—not related to a relationship gone awry but because I'd felt like somehow I'd gotten on the wrong track toward a destination that didn't fulfil me. I'd tried to plan things down to a microlevel, and that had blown up in my face. But my choices then had led me to my current life in

Ribbon, my marriage to Nick, and my relative satisfaction with how things had unfolded.

They also landed me on a dude ranch. Maybe a *little* planning was in order.

Kathy continued. "For a long time, Joey was my best friend. Those feelings don't just go away when you decide to get a divorce. I thought we'd stay in touch but live separate lives. Now..." Her voice trailed off. She looked down at her boots and wiped her eyes with her thumb and forefinger. When she looked back up, sadness was in her expression. "Now I've got to put aside my need to mourn his life and be strong for the rest of the employees here. Can you understand that?"

I nodded. On a whim, I reached out and grabbed her hand and squeezed. It was intended as a show of support, but Kathy must have been less touchy-feely than I was because she pulled away. As if realizing how odd her behavior was, she apologized.

"I'm sorry. I'm jumpy. It's taking everything I have to keep it together over the past few days. Last night, I took two sleeping pills to shut out the world, and I overcompensated with caffeine this morning."

"You've been through a lot," I said spontaneously. "Point me in the right direction, and I'll handle the laundry for you."

The orange-and-white cat appeared to recognize how ridiculous it was to trust me with a domestic task, but I was looking forward to it. I was finally being given some responsibility, and heading back into town might lead me to more information. (Not that I wanted to perform a forensic examination on the ranch's sheets, but you never know what you're going to find when you have access to dirty laundry.)

I followed Kathy back inside. The cowboys had dispersed. Nick was asleep on the reclining chair by the fire, and Senior was playing cards with Angus at the dining room table. Loncar, Tully, Chef, and Cody weren't anywhere to be seen.

Kathy lifted a set of keys from a hook by the door. "Take my car," she said. "The laundry is already loaded in the back seat. Henna is expecting someone from the ranch to bring our loads in today. She'll help you unload the bags when you get there."

"Henna? Tully's niece?"

"You already met her? Good. She works at the industrial laundry service in town. I'll call ahead and let her know you're on your way." She dropped the keys into my palm. "Don't forget to talk up the concert. We could all use a distraction."

After collecting my wallet, sunglasses, and phone, I went out front. Angus had driven Kathy's SUV around to the front and left it idling. I peered through the windows and saw several large plastic bags filled with soiled laundry in the back. Each bag was knotted closed and tagged with a label that said Down Home Ranch. The tags contained counts—one of five, two of five, three of five, etc.—and under those were piece counts of that bag's contents. I wasn't going to be able to just untie the bags and examine the contents without someone knowing.

"Everything okay?" called a voice behind me. I turned around and saw Angus approach.

"Yes." I pointed to the back seat. "I wanted to see what I was transporting."

"Bedding, mostly. Sheets, comforters, blankets. Towels and tablecloths too."

"What about clothes? You guys seem to get dirty."

"Exactly why we don't wash our work clothes regularly." He winked. "Life on the ranch is a lot simpler than what you're used to."

Simple wasn't the word I'd use to describe it, but to each his own.

Angus gave me directions to the laundromat, and I left. I couldn't shake the feeling that I was being sent away for reasons other than the ones in the back of the SUV, and despite my willingness to pitch in and help out, this task was getting me out of the way. Sending me into town alone was a good way to keep me from finding out anything more about what was going on.

It was a straight shot to the laundromat. Like the other day when Nick and I drove into town, the street-side parking had not yet filled, and after a U-turn, I found a spot in front of the laundromat entrance. Henna came out front. She seemed surprised to see me.

"Hey, girl," she said. "Samantha, right?"

"Right."

"Kathy said she was sendin' somebody with the wash, but when I saw the SUV, I expected Angus."

"Why's that?"

"She doesn't let anybody else drive her car."

It took me a moment of fussing with the buttons on the key before figuring out which one popped the hatch, but as soon as I did, Henna reached inside and yanked two Hefty bags out of the truck. She set them on the sidewalk and reached back in for two more. "Y'all can take off as soon as I get these unloaded."

"It's just me."

"Huh?"

"You said 'y'all,' but there's no 'all.' It's just me. Besides, you're from New Jersey. Why are you saying y'all?"

"It's an expression," she said with no trace of twang. "Fits my brand." She grinned, and I had to grin back. "Still, you don't have to stick around. I've got this."

"It feels good to help," I said.

"Suit yourself."

Henna pulled out the last of the bags and closed the hatch. She grabbed one in each hand and carried them inside. I tried to do the same thing and found I lacked the upper-body strength to carry two bags at once. I set one down and wrapped my arms around the other, leaned back, and hoisted it up. It was a struggle, but eventually I got it inside (in the same amount of time it took Henna to come back out and carry in two more bags). (Henna probably looked good in sleeveless dresses.)

When we finished, I followed her back into the laundromat. "Is that it?" I asked. "I can stick around and help you with the laundry if you want. An extra set of hands will help you get it done faster, right?"

"Nothing else to do today?"

"Yes, but don't you want to finish up early? Clear the decks so you can get ready for the concert this weekend? You're coming, right?"

"There ain't gonna be a concert this weekend," she said.

"Yes, there is. The singer arrived last night, and his band is coming today. They sing Willie, Waylon, and Cash."

"Pretty mainstream for here."

"I heard they're good. I, for one, am looking forward to hearing them."

She finished logging the bags into her ledger and slammed the book shut. "Doesn't matter how good the band is. Word about Joey's murder got out. I don't know what Kathy's thinking, trying to cover it up with a last-minute concert. We got fools around here, but there ain't nobody fool enough to party at the Down Home now."

21

MORE COMFORTABLE AROUND
HORSES THAN PEOPLE

"BUT THE WHOLE TEAM IS GETTING THE PLACE READY," I said. "I even helped Chef with the menu."

"Sorry to burst your bubble," Henna said. "Bummed me out too. Joey used to let me perform in the arena on concert nights. Give the early birds some rodeo fun before they headed inside for the music."

"Kathy told you not to do that?"

"Don't know. Didn't ask. Doesn't seem right, though. She should show some respect." She pulled her red hair behind her and knotted it with a ponytail holder she'd had around her wrist. "Everybody agrees."

"Everybody?"

"My uncle says it's wrong, the way she's pretending nothing happened."

It was obvious that Henna lacked respect for Kathy. If she knew the real reason Kathy was trying to keep the ranch running after the tragedy, she didn't let on. Kathy had said the ranch employees knew about her pending divorce from Joey, but it didn't seem that Henna was part of that group. I didn't know if it was my place to tell her or if doing so was spreading gossip that would make things more difficult for everyone.

"How's your uncle taking it?" I asked, switching the subject. "He knew Joey for a long time."

"Hard," she said. "Joey was his boss, but sometimes it felt like it was the other way around. Tully's been there so long he knows the place inside and out. When Joey took over, Tully was the one who taught him how to run the place."

"Is that what Tully told you?"

"He didn't have to tell me. I was there."

"You had to have been a kid."

"Doesn't mean I didn't see what was going on. I've been riding horses since I was four."

"Mysti said something about that."

"She'd know. She's been there since the beginning too."

I knew I'd been sent into town to drop off laundry and spread the word about the concert, but if Henna was right, then there wasn't much point in sacrificing myself on the altar of publicity. And what was waiting for me at the Down Home? Best-case scenario—I'd finish Chapter One. More likely, I'd be relegated to a bullshit task to keep me occupied while everybody else went about their ranch business. I wasn't itching to get back now that I suspected someone had reason to keep their eyes on me. Talking to Henna was a welcome break.

"Which beginning? When Joey took over as ranch manager?"

"I meant the beginning of my riding career. Tully used to train me in the early mornings and late afternoons. Joey saw how good I was and offered to stake me. He paid for everything— my registration fees, riding gear, and transportation. Tully trained me. I won my first blue ribbon when I was six."

"I can't imagine being on a horse at six."

"I'm more comfortable around horses than I am around people." She tore the tag off one of the bags and dumped the contents into a large laundry bin. She made a note in a ledger and slid the tag from the bag between the pages.

"How long did that arrangement last?" I asked.

"It never ended," she said. "Tully was training me to go on the circuit this year. Guess I'll be holding on to this job for the foreseeable future." Henna removed another tag and dumped the contents into a dingy yellow laundry cart on top of the first pile.

"My offer stands," I said, pointing to the cart. "Free labor," I added, pointing to me.

"If the owners find out I let a customer help me do my job, they'll fire me. I don't know what's going to happen next, but I *do* know I need this paycheck."

"Okay, then I guess I'll head back to the ranch." I

pointed over my shoulder with my thumb. Henna tackled a third bag, and I turned to leave.

"Hey, Samantha," Henna called out when I reached the door. I turned around. "Thanks for your offer. I don't get a lot of that." She smiled, and this time it felt genuine and not laced with sadness or forced to cover for deeper emotions. "Do you want to go out on a ride with me tomorrow morning? I promise I'll let you set the pace."

I grinned. "I'd love that," I said, surprised to discover it was the truth.

I left the laundromat and got back into Kathy's SUV but didn't start the engine. Everything Henna had said sounded plausible, but I couldn't dismiss the fact that she'd been at the ranch the morning I found Joey's body. She said she came to practice, but if her horse was in the stables, then she would have had to go in to get him ready to ride. I didn't know everything involved in that, but I knew horses didn't saddle up themselves.

I also had a new connection between Henna and Joey. She'd said he staked her from the time she was four, but what exactly was involved in that? Was a four-year-old capable of handling the pressures of competition, or had something happened back then that resulted in repressed trauma—something that maybe had come to the surface recently?

I glanced to my left into the windows of the laundromat and watched Henna. She was on her phone. Thirty seconds ago, she'd been concerned about how it would look to her employers if she let me pitch in, but considering she'd just been given five Hefty bags full of ranch laundry, she didn't seem particularly engaged in her job responsibilities. Maybe it was an innocent call—or maybe something I'd said had hit too close to home. Maybe I'd rattled her.

Regardless of my shifting plans for the day, I thought it best to move the car from out front and let Henna think I left town. I pulled out of my parking spot and drove down the road. Along the way I passed a couple of dueling steakhouses and a small white building with a sign labeling it the Marion Morrison Museum of Cowboy Memorabilia. I chuckled under my breath at that, still somewhat amused by the novelty of western ephemera, especially in New Jersey.

I kept driving, eventually reaching the sheriff's office. I coasted past it, playing out the pros and cons of dropping in and trying to talk things through with Parker. A soccer ball rolled in front of the SUV, and I slowed to a stop and waited while some kids ran out and grabbed it. To my right was a small lawn sign that said Bet on John Maverick for Sheriff next to a picture of two beer mugs clinking together.

Something about the sign didn't track with what I knew. In fact, the only Maverick I'd heard about was the manager of the Boot Strap, something I'd remembered as I cruised through the intersection past the bar. I drove to the next intersection in the left lane, preparing for my turn, but this was New Jersey and all left turns were made from the jughandle on the right. I drove about a half mile down the road before I was able to turn around.

I missed Pennsylvania.

The Boot Strap sat at the back of a gravel-covered parking lot. I pulled in and parked in a space close to the door. There was a hitching post out front, but no horses were tethered to it. Until three days ago, I would have said it was an ironic architectural detail to help sell the cowboy theme to tourists. Today, I knew otherwise.

I've been in a lot of odd situations, and many of them have raised my pulse rate. Walking into a cowboy bar by myself was among them. I glanced down at my jeans—Loncar's jeans—and tried to channel his former-homicide-cop demeanor then pulled the door open and went inside. Counters that displayed barbecued brisket and a variety of side dishes were on my right. I smiled at the young woman behind the counter and asked if Maverick was there. She directed me to the bar, and I moved farther inside.

The interior of the Boot Strap was dark, thanks to the knotty pine walls and the layer of peanut shells on the floor. I clomped toward the bar, sending discarded shells to the left and right as they ricocheted off the tips of my cowboy boots. A few crunched under my soles. A man in a black T-shirt wiped the bar down as I approached.

I didn't belong, and I knew it. I felt awkward and uncomfortable and as if a bouncer were going to appear and tell me I had no business being in a cowboy bar. And you know something? If that had happened, I would have happily left. Nothing was particularly threatening about the interior, but all the same, I was out of my element.

"Hi," I said. "Is Maverick here?"

"Depends who's asking," the man said. He kept wiping down the counters as if that were far more important than conversing with me.

"Yo, Mav," a woman behind me called across the interior. "We're running low on slaw. I'm going to the kitchen to make a new batch for tonight."

I'd suspected the man behind the bar was Maverick, and that was enough to confirm it. I'd turned my back on him when the woman called out his name, and when I turned back, I caught him staring at my jeans. He shifted his eyes up to my face, but not fast enough for me to guess he'd been checking me out. What might normally have annoyed me served the purpose of making me feel less out of place. His actions bolstered my confidence enough to get me to pull out a barstool and sit.

"What can I get ya?" he asked.

"Do you have sarsaparilla?"

"Only person who orders sarsaparilla in the Boot Strap is Sheriff Parker when he's on duty. You working for him?"

"No," I said quickly. "I'll have a…" I tried to remember what Rip drank on *Yellowstone*. Was it Coors or Budweiser? Or did they drink whiskey? I was *pretty* sure the cowboys drank beer. "What do you have on tap?"

"Shiner," he said.

"Sure. I'll take one of those."

He grabbed a glass and held it at an angle while cold yellow beer slid down the side. He righted it toward the end, and a foamy head filled the top of the glass. He set the mug on a coaster and pushed it toward me.

Maverick pulled out a second glass and filled it with soda.

"For a second there, I thought the sheriff sent in a spy. He hasn't been around here much since I announced my run for sheriff. Almost like he took it personally."

"I definitely don't work for the sheriff." I picked up my beer and sipped. The cold beverage slid down my throat easily, and I swallowed three gulps before remembering I hadn't eaten since my breakfast with Chef. Almost instantly, I felt a buzz radiate through me. My arms felt more relaxed, and the edge of nervousness I'd felt since walking in faded ever so slightly.

"Haven't seen you around before. You new to the area?"

"Visiting," I said. "I'm staying at the Down Home Ranch."

"You're not Lulu, are you?" He made a gesture toward his shirt. "Thought you'd be a little more blinged-out."

Having met Lulu, I laughed. "She does have a blingy wardrobe." I took another sip. "I'm Sam."

I don't know why I gave him a nickname. I generally don't like when people take liberties with my name and shorten it, especially when they barely know me. It felt like an assumption of familiarity that people have to earn. But between my nerves and the beer, I'd granted that familiarity to Maverick without a second thought.

Maybe it was because he acted like I belonged. Or maybe I needed an alter ego. Maybe Samantha was a city mouse who wore designer clothes and drank wine, but Sam was comfortable on a barstool in Jersey in her Wranglers and cowboy boots, drinking beer with a bartender.

There was something instantly likeable about Maverick. He had thick gray hair pulled back in a ponytail and a mustache. His upper body was lean and toned, like Patrick Swayze in *Road House*. I pictured him doing tai chi shirtless while the sun came up and felt my face heat to a degree that was probably visible. This whole cowboy thing was getting out of control.

"How long have you been riding?" Maverick asked.

"Me? What makes you think I ride?"

"The wear marks on your jeans," he said. "Don't tell me you stole them from a cowboy. I didn't take you for a buckle bunny."

"I'm definitely not one of those." I spun my glass around in a circle. The coaster underneath it was square, and it moved with the glass. "Why'd you think I was Lulu?"

"Joey told me about Billy and Lulu. Said it was an experiment. With what happened, I didn't think they'd stick around."

"I think they might have left early if she didn't have the accident."

"I was talking about Joey. What accident?"

"Lulu's horse threw her yesterday. She was in the arena, and she miscalculated a jump. He tossed her over his head. The doctor wanted to keep her in the hospital overnight just to make sure she didn't have a concussion."

Maverick stared at me intently, and I shifted uncomfortably. I took another swig of beer to hide my discomfort. "What are you doing in my bar?" he asked.

"I'm having a drink." I held up my empty glass. Drinking quickly on an empty stomach wasn't a good idea, but at least it backed up my story that the drink was why I was there.

"I heard you ask for me. Figured you came here for something other than the beer. Maybe it's time you told me what that is."

Something I'd said had shifted the energy between the bar manager and me, and my mind was just foggy enough to keep me from figuring out what it was. I had to win back his trust, and the way I saw it, there were two paths toward that—dishing dirt on Sheriff Parker or telling him the truth.

I went with the truth.

"Kathy sent me into town with the laundry. She asked me to spread the word about Saturday night's concert while I was here. I saw your sign outside the sheriff's office, and I got curious about you, so I came in here."

"My sign doesn't mention the Boot Strap. How'd you know to find me here?"

"One of the band members told me about you."

Maverick's face broke out in a wide grin. "You're Charlie's friend? He said you might be stopping by. Hot damn, this calls for a couple of shots."

22

THE BOOT STRAP

Yes, Loncar had been the one to point me to the Boot Strap. He'd been the one to mention Maverick—the person to help me find a replacement act. But it was one thing to know he'd told *me* about *them* and quite another to learn he'd told Maverick about *me*.

What had he said?

How had he described me?

Did Maverick know I was wearing Loncar's jeans?

Did he think we were sleeping together?

My face got hot again.

I protested the idea of shots, but apparently you can't refuse free booze in a cowboy bar, not when you're drinking with the manager who also happens to know the man who told him about you, the man whose jeans you're wearing, the man you walked into the bar to promote. Loncar had never told me how he knew

Maverick, and now did not seem the time to bring up the whole Batman-and-Robin thing.

Maverick pulled out two shot glasses and filled each from a bottle of bourbon. I regretted taking on an alter ego, but something told me Sam the cowgirl drank shots of bourbon regularly. Maverick handed me a shot glass, and he clinked his against mine. He tossed his back, and I swallowed mine in tiny chugs. The liquid burned the back of my throat and left me feeling like one of those circus people who swallows fire. Maverick had refilled my beer, and I reached out for my mug and swallowed a large gulp. I was on a one-way train toward disaster.

"Water?" I choked out.

Maverick laughed. He filled a red plastic tumbler and set it on the bar next to my beer. I pushed the beer away and pulled the water glass close, but my stomach was a churning blend of beverages, and the idea of adding anything other than food on top of the mix was less than appealing.

Maverick took a basket of peanuts and set it on the bar in front of me. I attacked the peanuts and got through about four before realizing he'd already refilled our shot glasses.

"I can't," I said. "I have to drive back."

"Too late for that now." He held out a second shot glass, and when I reluctantly took it, he clinked his against it. What the heck, I thought, and downed this one too. It was less burney than the first one, but the fact that

I'd just thought *burney* was an actual word told me my wits might be compromised.

I didn't care. The alcohol had relaxed me to a point that I hadn't felt since leaving Ribbon. While Nick and Senior and everybody else were having the time of their life on the ranch, I'd been a ball of stress from the moment we departed, which was fourteen hours before I'd expected to depart. Concerns about the reality of Senior investing in a dude ranch had given way to being the flat tire on the wagon wheel of fun.

There was no way I was leaving the Boot Strap anytime soon, not until I could pass a breathalyzer test. I shifted my weight on the barstool and cracked open a peanut shell. I tossed the shells on the floor and ate the nut, then cracked open another. Maverick leaned back against the center of the bar with the beer taps on his left. He crossed his arms over his T-shirt and watched me attack the nuts like they were my first meal after having been stranded on a desert island. It seemed maybe, as long as there were only two of us hanging out at the bar, I should try to converse. Otherwise, I was just a barfly.

I racked my brain for a decent topic of conversation and came up with "How long have you known Charlie Loncar?"

"You go first," Maverick said.

"We go way back. What about you?"

Maverick refilled my basket of peanuts. "We got arrested together. Drug deal at a gay bar in Philly. Cops brought in everybody until they could figure what was what."

"Loncar isn't... I mean... Drugs? A gay bar? Philly?"

"Probably happened before you two met."

Maverick reached forward and plunged his hands into a basin of soapy water. He pulled out a glass, rinsed it, and dried it with a towel. He set the clean glass on the counter behind him and started on another. I couldn't tell if he was truly that absorbed in the task of washing the barware or if it was a welcome distraction from my question, but at least it gave me something to watch.

Then there'd been the murder. Anybody could have found Joey's body in the stables, but it had been me. And from that moment, I'd slipped into my comfort zone. I'd gone right into that mode where, instead of making friends, I kept everybody at arm's length while I observed their behavior and slotted them into columns—innocent bystander or possible murderer. But aside from Nick, his dad, and now Loncar, I didn't know these people. Every single one of them *could* have murdered Joey for a variety of reasons, and that was the most troubling aspect of all. One person *had* killed Joey, and that meant every other one of them was at risk. I was no longer at a place of needing to find the killer; I needed to find my allies. I needed backup.

Yes! I needed backup!

"Where's your restroom?" I asked Maverick, pleased to hear that I wasn't yet slurring my words.

He pointed behind me, and I turned and saw the

word Ladies spelled out on a door in rope. I slowly eased myself off the stool and crunched my way through peanut shells until I was behind the door. I flipped the flimsy latch and phoned Nick. He didn't answer.

Maverick was right. It was too late for me to think about driving Kathy's SUV back to the ranch. I was beyond buzzed. I was on my way to passing out.

I hung up and sent Nick and Loncar a text: *Doing shots at the boot strap. Need ride.*

When I came out of the ladies' room, I was no longer the only patron in the bar. A few tables had filled with cowboys in various shades of bandana-printed shirts behind aluminum trays of sliced brisket, white bread, and pickles. Someone had turned up the music, and the sounds of conversation mingled with somebody singing about his truck, or his tractor, or his horse. (With country music, sometimes it's hard to keep track.) (Cowboys *did* seem to have strong feelings toward their modes of transportation.)

I went back to my barstool and ate seven more peanuts then finished off my tumbler of water. Maverick was on the other side of the bar, talking to a couple of college-aged guys in hoodies. I checked my phone obsessively, hoping for a reply from one of the men in my life. Wherever they were, they did not seem to be checking their phones with any intensity.

A few minutes later, a second bartender came over to check on me. "You okay?"

"I'm waiting for my ride."

"You want another shot?"

"Just the check."

I cashed out and sat on my stool for a few more minutes. It was after four, and the happy-hour crowd was steadily filling the place. There was a serious deficit in the cowgirl-to-cowboy ratio, which made me feel even more conspicuous, though for a time, none of the men around me seemed to care that I was there.

Whatever silence had allowed Maverick and me to converse had been replaced with the raucous laughter that comes from letting off steam at the end of an honest day's work, and my alter-ego identity slipped away, and the out-of-place feeling returned. I pulled out a couple bills and left them on the bar. If Nick wasn't going to swoop in on a white horse, then I was going to have to walk off my buzz. The sun had already started to descend, and I didn't particularly feel like wandering around the mean streets of New Jersey after dark.

I finished my tumbler of water. A rodeo clown came in through the back door. It creeped me out how this town was crawling with them, and as conspicuous as I felt, I didn't want to give him a chance to make me a target. I stood up on wobbly legs and made my way out the door in search of a way to sober myself up.

23

NOT MEANT FOR THE COWBOY LIFE

NICK FOUND ME SITTING ON THE CURB OUTSIDE A LITTLE Caesars. On my knees rested a pizza box with three pieces missing, two of which were in my stomach and one of which was in my hands. The fog of alcohol had left my system, thanks to the two hours that had passed since I left the Boot Strap, the mile I'd walked in my boots, and the pizza I'd consumed.

Nick settled in on the curb next to me. He didn't say anything. He removed a slice and bit into it.

"I'm not meant for the cowboy life," I said dejectedly. "I can barely hold my liquor."

Nick chewed his first mouthful and swallowed then took another rather large bite and swallowed that one too. By his third bite, I started to think he didn't want to talk about me doing shots at the Boot Strap. By the time he took his fourth bite, I started to think Nick was tired of cowboy food too.

He finished his slice and took another. "I don't know how I should feel about you drinking at a gay cowboy bar instead of trying to find Joey's killer. That may be progress."

"The Boot Strap isn't a gay bar," I said, as if that would help me seem a little less reckless. I thought back to the interior, the casual confidence of Maverick, and the way the place had a dearth of women. "Is it?"

"It is."

"But Loncar sent me there. He knows Maverick, the bartender. When I mentioned Loncar's name, Maverick started pouring me shots."

"How many shots did you do?"

"Three," I said. "I think."

"You think?"

"It's a blur." I finished my third slice and contemplated a fourth.

(There was no contemplating. I knew I was going to take the fourth slice. Nick knew I was going to take the fourth slice. I'd like to pretend it was due to the bourbon and the extenuating circumstances, but the fact of the matter was that I like pizza.)

"Did anything interesting happen while I was gone?"

"Nothing out of the ordinary," Nick said. "I spent the afternoon helping Angus and Cody set up a stage and a temporary dance floor for tomorrow night."

"Where was Kathy?"

"Not sure. Why?"

"When I left, she said she had to stay at the ranch to

make sure the day-to-day business ran properly, that everybody was watching her to see how well she handled things now that Joey is gone."

"She's right."

"How do you know?"

"At first, the ranch staff acted like we were guests, but they couldn't keep that up. After two days of us pitching in and helping out with their work load, they dropped the niceties."

"What have they said?"

"Mainly that Kathy's in over her head. Word is out that she's looking to unload the ranch sooner rather than later."

"What does your dad think?"

"He's having the time of his life. I can't remember the last time I saw him look so alive."

"Is he seriously thinking about buying? After the murder? Does he have that kind of money to invest?"

"His shares in the shoe company are more than enough to buy the place and cover a budget for upkeep and one or two salaries."

That gave me pause. Nick wasn't the only one of us to notice how alive Senior seemed since arriving at the ranch. He'd become an honorary cowboy, going out on the morning rides, playing poker with the guys, and pitching in wherever necessary. I'd watched Angus, Tully, and Cody around him, and they seemed to treat him as if he'd been part of the ranch forever.

But years ago when I was first reinventing my life

from buyer of shoes at Bentley's New York to trend specialist for a now-defunct department store in Ribbon, Nick had initiated his own reinvention. At the time, Nick Taylor Designs, the company his dad had started, was under the umbrella of a parent company which provided the capital and pressured him to expand his distribution to an ever-expanding retail base. It was a partnership that worked on paper but kept Nick busy with business choices instead of creative ones. He eventually bought back controlling interest and chose to fund the entire operation himself. He'd had relationships with the media in place, and after he showed a stable growth trajectory, he'd had the luxury of turning away interested investors. After a taste of being his own boss, he found he liked it.

"Are you okay with your dad selling his shares in the company? That would leave you with an investment partner. You've done a lot to ensure that would never happen again."

"It wouldn't be just another partner. He wants to sell his shares to Blak Friiday."

Of course. It was the perfect solution.

A few years ago, Nick had diversified his designer shoe business by starting a sneaker line called Saint Nick. His early designs had caught the attention of a pro-football player turned hip-hop artist named Blak Friiday, and the two of them entered into a partnership. Their launch had broken all sorts of records for independent sneaker companies, and they'd been on the short list for collaborators of the year before a set of unusual circumstances had forced us to sacrifice that award to bait a bigger trap. What had emerged from that was a solid relationship between Nick and Blak, between Senior and Blak, and between me and Blak. If Nick was going to have an investment partner, I could think of no better choice.

"How does Blak feel about this?"

"He's a go. He's just waiting to see how this weekend unfolds."

"I'm surprised he didn't want to come along and see for himself."

"Blak says he's not the cowboy type."

"I know how he feels."

I finished my fourth slice and started to regret it. The dough sat in a ball in my stomach. I pulled a piece of pepperoni off a remaining slice (because at this point, why not?) and shifted the box to Nick's lap. He shifted it to the sidewalk on the other side of him, as if out of sight, out of mind would keep me from asking for more.

"How do you feel?" he asked.

"Now? Full. Sluggish. Like I could pass a breathalyzer."

"Good. No activities planned for tonight, so you'll be able to turn in early. I'll give you a ride back to the bar, and you can follow me back to the Down Home."

The parking lot of the Boot Strap was full. Two horses were tethered to the hitching post, answering my earlier question. Kathy's SUV was now hidden between two larger trucks, and I instructed Nick to leave the lot and wait for me on the street out front so I could follow him back.

In the time I'd been gone, someone had come through the lot and tucked promotional fliers under the windshield wipers. I pulled mine off and glanced at the paper. It advertised an upcoming trick rodeo show for the following weekend. I folded the flyer in half and in half again and jammed it into my pocket then concentrated on the task at hand. With any luck, we'd be long gone by then.

———

THE ATMOSPHERE at the Down Home was relaxed. One of the cowboys was asleep on the sofa by the fire. He had his hat resting over his face, but by the fancy embroidery on his shirt, I guessed it was Billy. I'd failed to ask Nick about Lulu's status, but if Billy was here and not at the hospital, then I assumed she was out of the woods.

Senior, Cody, Loncar, and Tully sat at the dining room table, playing cards.

"Hey, Kiddo," Senior called out. "Junior thought you found yourself a cowboy and ditched him."

"She found herself a pizza and ditched me," Nick said with a grin.

The saloon doors to the kitchen opened, and Chef came out. He held two large bowls of homemade Chex Mix, which he set on the table. "Hi, Samantha. You wanted a pizza? Not a lot of options in town. You should have said something. I can fire up the brick oven out back and have one ready in about five minutes."

"It was more out of necessity than craving." I glanced at Loncar. "I ran into one of Charlie's friends at the Boot Strap, and we did shots."

The other men around the table didn't even respond. I'd expected, once word got out about my afternoon with Maverick, to be the target of jokes at my expense, especially after learning what I had about the nature of the bar, but it was as if they hadn't even noticed I was gone. The afternoon might not have gotten me anything more than a throbbing headache, but it had provided a reprieve from being in everybody's way. Nothing says "you're not part of the group" like not being missed when you're gone.

Loncar kept his eyes on mine. I wanted to talk to him, to ask him about what Maverick had told me and find out the real story. I wanted to warn him that he was going to have to convince more than just the strangers around here that he was who he pretended to be.

Nick slung his arm around my shoulders. "Hey, Kidd, Angus is setting up a projector for movie night tonight. Do you want to go take a nap? You've got about an hour until the sun goes down."

No, I did not want to take a nap, and I almost flung Nick's arm off my shoulders and told him that. But I *did* want to take a nap. I wanted to sleep through the rest of this vacation. And I was feeling sorry enough for myself that I didn't care anymore about proving myself, about jumping in to help with the tasks like Nick, Loncar, and his dad had done. I was starting to understand why most westerns had almost entirely male casts. Aside from the one woman who held the whole place together, women didn't fit into this world.

Speaking of which… "Where's Kathy?"

"She's in the stables with Tully," Cody said, barely looking up.

"Is everything okay?"

This time he did look up. He set his cards face down on the table and studied me with an uncomfortable intensity. "Why wouldn't it be?"

This time I did shrug Nick's arm off my shoulder, not because Nick had anything to do with my response but because I'd had enough of the cowboy dismissiveness.

"Oh, I don't know, maybe it's because her husband was murdered in those stables. Or because one of the horses tossed a rider and sent her to the hospital. Or maybe because Tully and Kathy don't particularly like each other, and I can't see them choosing to spend time together if they don't have to."

Cody flicked the front of his hat, and it shifted onto the back of his head, revealing more of his face. He didn't respond to my outburst. The others continued to play their hands, moving chips from their individual piles of varying size to the pot in the center.

"Your bet, Cody," Senior said.

But Cody didn't seem to hear him. "Maybe you should mind your own business." He unfolded himself from his seat at the table and tossed his cards on the table. Without breaking eye contact with me, he said, "I fold." He stormed toward the front door and left the group.

I watched his back. Nick put his hands on my shoulders, as if wanting to keep me from following. But it was Senior who kept me where I was. He let out a long, low whistle.

"I don't know what he's bent out of shape over," Senior said. "Would you look at that? He had a full house."

I glanced back at the cards on the table. Cody had abandoned a pile of chips that would have bought him a brand-new Stetson, and I wanted to know why.

24

MISS POPULARITY

Nick bent his head and whispered in my ear. "No, you're not going after him."

"But he—"

Nick's fingers tightened on my shoulders. "No," he said, and this time it wasn't a suggestion.

Before I had a chance to process the practical reasons Nick might not want me to storm after a (possibly) shady cowboy with (possibly) something to hide, Mysti came over to the table.

"Hey, Samantha," she said. "I've been waiting for you to get back. I have something for you."

In the span of twenty-four hours, I'd gone from persona non grata to Miss Popularity, like a memo had circulated to make me feel welcome. I would have been suspicious if not for the fact that the shifting winds felt good.

Today the spiritual guide wore a long blue floral dress with her ivory-embroidered cowboy boots. The dirt from yesterday had been brushed from the boots, and the embroidery was bright and intricate. Her long, curly hair was tied into a low ponytail, and loose curls framed her cherubic face, which was a peachy-pink shade flushed with rosy cheeks.

"Something for me?" I perked up a bit. Aside from Chef, Mysti had the highest likelihood of being able to give me something I wanted.

"Yes. Are you busy?"

The pressure of Nick's hands on my shoulders went from holding me back to gently pushing me forward. I glanced at him, and he nodded. He leaned forward again and whispered, "Remember, we're doing this for my dad." He kissed me on the cheek.

I stood. "Nope, not busy. I was just thinking of resting up before movie night starts."

She rushed forward and grabbed my hand. "I've got something even better." Her hand closed around mine, and she pulled me toward her display. A small bundle wrapped in faded pink calico sat on her chair. A tag had been attached with beige grosgrain ribbon, and my name had been written on the tag. "For you." She grabbed the bundle with her free hand, but instead of handing it to me, she tucked it under one arm and pulled me outside.

"Where are we going?" I asked.

"My she-shed." She giggled. "No men allowed."

Any concerns I had about leaving the group melted away with that phrase. My world had been on a tilt since arriving. Having to relinquish all control to the men of the ranch was anything but relaxing. If Mysti took me to the bunkhouse and asked me to scrub the floor, I might say yes just to have a responsibility.

Fortunately, that wasn't her destination.

A small wooden shed sat on the ranch property in a field behind the main house. The exterior was sage green, and a mural of tall sunflowers had been painted on the exterior, as if they'd been planted in a rectangular plot to frame the structure with their bright-yellow blossoms. Mysti unlocked a padlock on the outside and held the door open, and when I stepped inside, I felt as if I'd entered an entirely different world.

Colorful abstract paintings hung on the walls, coordinating with a display of wooden Russian Matryoshka dolls displayed on the mantel. An ivory chenille sofa faced two orange chairs, modern in style. The seating arrangement, completed by a square glass coffee table, sat on a striped throw rug in bold shades of purple, orange, and yellow. The space was bold and energetic, nothing like what I expected.

Before I fully took in the rest of the interior, Mysti handed me the calico bundle she'd had under her arm. She approached a round dining room table and lit each in a grouping of candles that sat in the center. She hiked up the skirt portion of her dress and sat down then uncorked a bottle of red wine and filled a glass. "Would you like some wine?"

"I think I'll stick to water," I said, playing it safe and rehydrating after my day drinking with Maverick in town.

She picked up a carafe filled with water and lemon wedges, poured a glass, then handed it to me. "Have a seat. You're safe here."

"Safe from what?"

"Testosterone, for starters." She pulled her wineglass toward her and allowed herself a sip then set the glass back on the table.

"What is this place?" I scanned as much of it as I could, wondering how something that looked like a display out of *Modern Living* could coexist on a plot of the ranch.

"This is where I stay when I'm here," she said. "Chef has a room in the main house, but I'm not one for bunking under one roof with my husband's employers. I asked for a room to decorate as I saw fit, and they did me one better. Joey and Tully built it after Chef took the job."

"It doesn't look anything like the big house," I said, trying to keep my opinion about the ranch décor out of my voice.

"That was part of the deal." She winked. She sipped her wine then set down her glass and tapped the calico bundle. "Go on and open it."

I pulled on the edge of the string, and the fabric fell away from the contents. Inside was a basket with sage spray, a candle, and a small protection bracelet made of black beads.

I pulled the items out one by one and stacked them to the side. In addition, I found a card with meditations and a handful of rough crystals tied to smaller cards indicating their intent. It was everything you might expect to find in a spiritual gift basket, and there was a time when it might have been the best gift anybody ever gave me.

"Thank you," I said. The gesture was nice. Mysti had no way of knowing my ongoing quest for happiness had led me through the metaphorical sagebrush and into a place where I trusted my gut more than a deck of tarot cards.

"You know you don't need any of that," Mysti said with a sweeping gesture toward the pile.

"You're a spiritual guide," I said. "I'm pretty sure you're supposed to believe that I do."

"I believe in clearing our minds and understanding our truths," she said. "You already know your truth. I saw it in your eyes the moment I met you. You're very self-aware."

"I spent a lot of years thinking I didn't know what I knew." I picked up the sage spray to read the label then set the bottle back down. "I've gone through cases of this stuff. One time I sprayed Nick while he was sleeping."

"Why?"

"Protection. From me. I have a habit of getting mixed

up in situations that aren't always on the up-and-up, and I wanted to shield him from that."

"You already know you're not responsible for your husband's choices. You can accept him, and he can accept you, and that's the best thing love can offer us."

"Yes, but Nick hasn't always had a choice."

She held up her hand to silence me. "We always have a choice. We don't always use it."

I gave that a moment to sink in. It was a different way of looking at life—not from the vantage point of a victim who constantly got steamrolled by circumstance but from the perspective of control. If Mysti was right, then I'd been in the driver's seat all along.

"For as long as I can remember, I've been looking for something, but I didn't know what it was."

"Did you find it?"

I shrugged. "I got tired of looking, so I just sort of gave up and started living my life."

"And how did that make you feel?"

"Great. Until we showed up here. All of a sudden, I'm back in that corner where I need to find out how to fit into a world that doesn't seem to want me. I don't know what I'm doing here. I don't know how to be a cowgirl. Everywhere I go, I'm in the way. Every time I try to help out, I mess things up. Everybody here sees me as a nuisance."

"Like who?"

"Like Cody," I said. "There's something about him that puts me on edge. At first, I got a charge out of being flirted with by a cowboy. Trust me, that was as much of a surprise to me as to anybody! But he treats me like I'm helpless, and I'm not wired to accept that."

"Did something happen between you?"

"He told me Kathy was meeting with Tully, and when I asked if everything was okay, he acted like that was a crazy question. I listed all the reasons it was not only a reasonable question but why it was suspicious that nobody else was asking the same thing."

"What were those reasons?"

"That someone murdered Kathy's husband in the stables. That someone let out the horses that same night, possibly to cause a distraction. That Lulu had an accident in the arena the next day. That someone cut the fuel line of Tully's truck while Nick and I were in town. That the musical act canceled at the last minute."

"You mentioned all of that to Cody?"

"Some of it. Not all."

"What did he say?"

"He said I didn't know what I was talking about, and he stormed out of the room."

As I spoke, I spun the cobalt-blue bottle of sage spray between my hands. Mysti reached across the table, picked up the bottle, and set it at the end of the table out of my reach.

"How did that make you feel?"

"Like he knows something I don't, which, okay, I get it. That's not a stretch. For the first few days that we were here, I kept offering to pitch in, but everybody said they didn't need my help. Today, it's been the opposite. Chef asked me to help plan the menu for the party tomorrow, and Kathy sent me into town with the laundry, but instead of feeling like I'm helping out, I feel like the victim of a conspiracy to keep me out of the way."

"What about your husband and your father-in-law? Are they having the same experience?"

"Nick has spent a lot of time with Tully, and Senior's become an unofficial resident of the bunkhouse. They have no complaints, which makes me feel even more like an outsider."

"What did you see when you first got here? That first time you entered the big house, what were your initial thoughts about Angus and Cody?"

"Lumberjack extras in a Hallmark movie," I said, remembering my first impression of the two ranch hands.

"What do you think they saw when they looked at you?"

"I never considered what they thought."

"Then consider this. Everybody here wears a cowboy hat but you. The high crown provides insulation, and the wide brim shields you from the sun. And everybody here carries a bandana but you. It's possibly the single most useful accessory to have on hand, especially for covering your mouth when dirt is stirred up by the horses. Your boots are obviously brand-new, and you're the only woman here who bothers with lipstick. The thing that makes you look like you belong are your jeans, and I'm guessing they're not your jeans."

"I borrowed them from someone who knows the real me," I said in a voice that suggested I was embarrassed by her accurate assessment.

"If it was your husband, you would have said so. Judging from the wear pattern, I think I know who loaned them to you. Tell me, Samantha, does your husband know you're sleeping with the lead singer of the band?"

25

GUIDED TO TROUBLE

"It's not like that," I said. "I mean, it's a little like that. These are his jeans, but—"

I took a long, slow, deep inhale and let it out in a rush. It was the most clichéd response to frustration that existed, but it seemed like the thing to do when face-to-face with a spiritual guide who had included a wooden block that said *Breathe* in my gift basket.

"Charlie is a retired homicide detective," I said. "I met him years ago when he investigated a murder at my place of employment." (I left out the details that I was his main suspect at the time and that our initial meetings were less than friendly.) "Over the years, we've gotten to a place of trust."

"Everybody's got a past." Mysti tipped her head to the side and swept her curly hair over her shoulder. "Angus is an art scholar. He specializes in art of the American West. He used to teach at Temple University.

He'll never tell you that, but he has a doctorate in Fine Arts. Some days, when he's out there roping calves, he looks like he could be the subject of a C. M. Russell painting instead of the one who could tell you the history of it. Have you seen the painting over the mantel at the big house?"

I nodded. "The cowboy, right? It fits right in."

"It's an original Remington," she said. "Joey and Angus were on a road trip to go see about some horses. Angus spotted it on the curb on trash day. He suspected what it was and had Joey pull over. When they returned, he called in a team of experts from the Philadelphia Museum of Art to officially authenticate it."

"It was nice of Angus to let Joey put it on display. It sets the tone for the whole place."

"I don't think Joey ever thought of the painting as belonging to Angus. It was part of the ranch."

"How much is it worth?"

"More than this whole place," she said with a sweeping gesture.

I never would have taken Angus, the white-haired ranch hand, for a college-level professor of art, which spoke to both my first impression of him and my assessment that college professors were not the sort to get their hands dirty.

"What about Cody?" I asked. "Is he secretly a financial analyst or a yoga instructor?"

She smiled. "Cody used to travel on the rodeo circuit. He injured his hand in a roping accident and had to quit.

He got into some trouble around then, and Joey bailed him out."

"What trouble?"

"The kind that involves six months in a county jail. When I said Joey bailed him out, I meant it literally. A lot of people said Cody would never ride a horse again, and that put him in a bad place, but Joey didn't give up on him. It took six months of physical therapy, but once Cody started his rehabilitation, he never gave up. Now he's more a part of this ranch than any of us."

"So Cody didn't have any trouble with Joey?"

"I didn't say that." She seemed lost in her thoughts for a few seconds, and I watched her, wondering if she regretted telling me as much as she had or if she was carefully considering her next choice of words. "Joey had a domineering side. He wanted people to be there when he needed them, and when he needed them, he didn't think twice about asking. Except it wasn't always asking. He had a way of encouraging the people around him to get indebted to him. He leveraged their gratitude to get what he wanted."

"Is that what he did with Henna?"

"What do you mean?"

"She told me how Joey sponsored her on the rodeo circuit when she was a child. She's not a child anymore. I just wondered—"

"Joey had his faults, but I never saw him take advantage of a woman."

I leaned back and scanned the décor behind Mysti.

The exterior looked like what I might have expected, but the interior did not. "What about you?"

"I'm a trained psychologist. I had a practice in town, but cowboys and psychiatry aren't a natural fit. I changed my branding and labeled myself a spiritual healer."

"Doesn't that bother you? That you can't be what you were trained to be?"

"Why would it bother me? I want to help people. I found a way to help people. It's the same work but under a different guise."

I pulled the jet-black beaded bracelet out of the basket and slipped it on over my wrist. The beads were all black save for two—one blue and one tiger's-eye. The bracelet was pretty in a non-feminine, asexual way.

Each member of the ranch wore similar bracelets, and in some cases, they wore several stacked up against each other.

"Everybody here wears these," I said. "Why?"

"I offered them to the staff, and they took them. People come to the ranch and see the staff wearing protection bracelets and want to buy their own. I set up a table in the lobby and give half of what I make to Kathy."

"That makes Angus and Cody cowboy influencers."

She chuckled. "Something like that."

"They don't mind?"

"The money goes back into the ranch. That makes their lives more comfortable. It's a symbiotic circle."

"So it's not about the bracelet?"

"It's not about the bracelet. It's also not about candles

or sage or feng shui. It's about believing that everything will be okay. Maybe you can't see the big picture, but that doesn't mean the big picture can't see you. It's about taking your hands off the reins and knowing you're always being guided."

"That's easy for you to say. Most of the time, it feels like I'm being guided to trouble."

"Maybe in another timeline, you're a cop. Or a detective. Or a spirit guide. Maybe you're a medium who assists the souls of the deceased to reach the afterlife." She paused for a few seconds and took another sip of her wine. "Or maybe you're a problem solver with a nose for trouble."

"That's what I am now."

"Is that so bad?"

No, it wasn't. But it also meant I knew what I had to do.

I thanked Mysti for the gift, though we both knew the true gift she'd given me wasn't a basket of items of spiritual intent but a peek behind the curtain into her anti-ranch life. Everything I'd seen from the moment we arrived had been fed to me as part of an experience. Not all had been as it seemed, but I'd taken it at face value. Talking to her, I had a better understanding of the people who'd tended to us since we arrived. They were no longer caricatures of dude ranch employees to me. They were real people with real histories and real motivations. They had dreams and aspirations and setbacks like the rest of us. Maybe I was here because Senior was thinking about buying the place, but even if he did, it would be an investment property that he visited from time to time. To the employees, working at the Down Home wasn't like clocking in for a shift at Dunder Mifflin. It was their way of life.

I left Mysti's She Shed and walked back toward the house. Lights were on in the kitchen, making it easy to follow the straight line back to the house. Tully was on the right side of the house, at the back of two rows of picnic benches. The interior light illuminated his red hair, making him easy to track. He stood next to a projector, with a coil of thick black cord in one hand. There wasn't much light on this side of the building, and Tully seemed to be having a difficult time seeing what he was doing.

Bolstered by my conversation with Mysti, I approached him. We'd shared few words since my arrival, but now more than ever, I felt much of that was my fault. I called out a greeting. Tully glanced up at me but didn't respond. I strode to where he stood and grabbed the thick cord out of his hand. The coil was heavier than I thought, and I needed both hands to keep from dropping it. I readjusted and hooked it over my elbow then used the other hand to keep it supported.

Tully glanced at my hands then pulled a flashlight out of his pocket and aimed the beam at the projector. He located the plug, fit the end of my cord into the machine, and turned it on. A flickering image appeared on the exterior wall. He appeared to be satisfied with the outcome. He switched off the projector and took the cord from me, laying it on the ground.

"Thanks," he said. "I prefer horses to machines, but there's nobody else around to set this contraption up."

"Where are Angus and Cody?" I asked.

"Kathy took Angus into town," he said. "Cody's out with the group on a late-night ride."

This was more conversation than Tully and I had exchanged since I arrived, and while it wasn't overwhelmingly friendly, it wasn't hostile either.

"I'm sorry about your truck," I offered.

"You the one who cut the fuel line?"

"No! Of course not."

"Then no point apologizing for something you didn't do."

"What *did* I do?" I asked.

He stared at me, as if not understanding the question.

"To make you dislike me," I continued. "I get that I'm not a natural out here on the ranch, but I've done nothing but try to be friendly. I didn't set the horses free the night Joey was murdered, and I wasn't the one who killed him. You act like I had a hand in both of those tragedies."

Tully crossed his arms. "You remind me of my ex-wife."

Of all the things he could have said, that answer was the least expected. "What?"

"She liked to sit by the fire and read westerns too." He pulled off his cowboy hat and set it on the folding chair next to him. "Her favorites were the ones by Louis L'Amour."

"If it's any consolation, I don't usually sit around reading westerns," I said. "I thought they would help get me into the spirit of the trip."

"Seems to me the spirit of the trip is to decide if we're worth our asking price."

Tully may have blamed his dislike of me on my resemblance to his ex, but this seemed like the real crux of the problem. "You're not happy that Joey and Kathy put the place up for sale," I surmised.

"Not sure Joey had all that much to say about it."

"It was his ranch. It's been in his family for generations."

"He and I had an informal agreement. He knew his wife didn't want the place. He said he was going to leave it to me to run as I saw fit. He had the paperwork all drawn up, just needed to file it."

"You saw it?"

"Sure, I saw it. He needed my signature to make it official. Awfully funny how it went missing shortly after he died."

"But what about Kathy? Why wouldn't he leave the ranch to her?"

"She doesn't want this place. Never has. She got a hefty golden parachute when she was let go from her advertising job. Between that and the painting, she's set."

"But that painting belongs to Angus." I didn't know if

that was common knowledge, but Tully didn't seem surprised that I knew.

"Possession is nine-tenths of the law, ma'am." He picked his hat back up and set it on top of his red hair. "Don't you forget it."

While Tully and I talked, the scent of freshly popped corn filled the air. Billy and Lulu rounded the back of the building, each weighed down with large bowls overflowing with fluffy kernels. Billy carried two bowls, one in each hand. Lulu was behind him with two more. Chef came out the back door of the kitchen with a tray of spices. Billy and Lulu lined up their bowls on the picnic table next to pitchers of beer, and Chef set the spice tray next to them. Billy and Lulu returned to the back of the building while Chef arranged the spices.

"Is this still left over from earlier in the week?" I asked Chef.

"Nope. Mashed that up and served it to the chickens." He jutted his chin toward Lulu and Billy. "You've got them to thank for this."

Lulu smiled. "I got tired of lying around recovering from my accident while everybody else had fun." She set her bowls down and went back inside.

"But the kettle is cool," I said, pointing to the large cast-iron pot behind Billy. "We would have heard if you used it to make all of this."

Billy looked embarrassed and glanced at the back door, through which Lulu had gone. "Lulu saw Chef use lard in the kettle. She's vegan. We bought up a load of vegetable oil and spent the last two hours popping corn over the skillet in the bunkhouse. Thought that would be quieter than doing it here."

"I thought women weren't allowed in the bunkhouse." It was a minor point, but it was worth noting.

"Angus made an exception," Billy said. "He's a sucker for kettle corn."

That explained why we hadn't heard the popping.

"Maybe I'll try something new tonight," I said. "How do you like it, Chef?"

Chef shrugged. "By the time I've got the kettle cleaned out, I'm usually not in the mood for popcorn. Billy and Lulu gave me the night off, and I'm going to enjoy it."

Lulu came back with two more bowls of popcorn. "Help yourself," she said. "We've been popping for hours. There's plenty to go around."

I am not the sort who needs to be told twice when it comes to salty snacks, so I reached toward one of the bowls. Nick came out of the kitchen and called my name before I could take any popcorn. He carried a bowl, too, but he kept his with him. He held out his hand to me, and I took it and followed him to the back row of seats.

"Don't you need to put that on the table with the rest of the popcorn?" I asked.

"You said you're not much for kettle corn. Don't tell anybody, but I popped this in the microwave just for you."

"You mean just for *us*," I corrected.

"Nope. That's all yours. I'm going to try the cowboy-spice combination. Achiote, meat tenderizer, and pulverized dry black beans." He took the bowl of popcorn from my lap and held it out of my reach. "Unless you want to try that too?"

I leaned forward and grabbed the bowl. "If you want to eat that, that's on you." I pulled the bowl toward me and rested it on my lap. I grabbed a handful of corn and ate a few kernels. It was salty, buttery, and darn near perfect. I settled in for the evening's entertainment. "Where's Loncar?" I asked while I chewed.

"He went into town. Wanted to meet Sheriff Parker before tomorrow night."

I hadn't had time to tell Loncar what Henna had said at the laundromat, that nobody was going to come to a party at the Down Home after Joey's murder, but I doubted that would have stopped Loncar. He liked to operate on the up-and-up, and he trusted law enforcement personnel to do their jobs. He'd have a better chance at helping the town sheriff if he came clean about his identity instead of confusing the waters by hiding behind a guitar and a microphone.

As much as I should have enjoyed movie night on the ranch, I wasn't able to clear my mind. My conversation with Mysti replayed on a loop. I'd pegged everybody here as being what they seemed, but the truth had been the biggest surprise. From the moment we arrived, I allowed the atmosphere of the ranch to inform my observations. I wrote off Cody and Angus as uneducated, assumed Mysti was flighty, and expected our meals to be beef, beef, and beef. It wasn't until I heard Kathy mention the vegan menu planned for Lulu that I even considered that there would be a Michelin-star chef on hand to make whatever we wanted, and even then, I kept what I wanted to myself. I'd played along with the cowboy concept as if I were a guest at a goofy theme party.

But the people who ran the ranch didn't think of this life as a joke. Angus had walked away from an intellectual career at a museum to handle the physical aspects of this job, and Cody had found a path forward that included an honest day's work and a form of rehabilitation for his injuries. Henna, who held down a job at a laundromat in town, considered training in the arena as her real job. And Tully was so much of a Down Home fixture that Joey, faced with the reality of not having another generation to hand down the place to, had viewed Tully as the wise choice to be custodian of the family property.

But someone here was hiding something. Somebody knew what Joey's true intentions had been and wanted to make sure they wouldn't be seen through.

Despite the darkness, the flickering movie light made it easy to take inventory of the people seated outside. Billy and Lulu sat in the front row. Cody was between Tully and Senior on a bench on the opposite side of the projector, and Chef sat behind them with his arm around Mysti. Henna had joined the group and was a few feet away from Mysti. Aside from Kathy and Angus, the gang was all here.

"Where's Angus?" I whispered to Nick.

"He drove Loncar into town."

Which meant nobody was inside the house.

I moved my bowl of popcorn to Nick's lap. "I'll be right back," I said.

"Where are you going?"

"Bathroom."

Nick nodded. I left my seat and went into the main house. It was quiet. The crocheted afghan had been neatly folded on the leather sofa, and the fireplace was dark. Wall sconces provided enough light for me to see where I was going but not by much. I would have loved the benefit of a bright overhead light, but turning one on would indicate where I was, and if I wanted to be sneaky, then the last thing I needed was to draw attention. I crept through the house toward the base of the staircase. I hadn't been upstairs since we arrived. Kathy slept up there. So did Chef and, since his arrival, Loncar. I knew exactly what secret Loncar hid, but Kathy? Not so much.

I crept up the stairs and slipped into the first room on the left. It was vacant. The mattress had been stripped of linens, and the wastepaper basket was empty. I left that room and checked out two more, finding them in similar states. Loncar's quarters were easy enough to identify thanks to his guitar case. I checked the last two rooms. They, too, showed no signs of having been inhabited.

It was possible that Chef stayed with Mysti, especially

when the big house was filled with guests and a potential murder suspect. There was no way Nick would let me sleep alone under similar circumstances. But none of these rooms appeared to belong to Kathy. She should, by all accounts, be sleeping in the master suite, but it was as bare as the rest of the vacant rooms. It wasn't just the lack of linens—explained by the five bags of laundry I'd taken into town—but something else. If Kathy were living out of one of these rooms, there would be evidence of her presence—a shirt over the back of a chair, a pair of shoes tucked under the bed, a cord to charge a cell phone, a book on the nightstand. Something.

As I stood on the landing, thinking about what this meant, I saw movement downstairs. I ducked and froze in place. I couldn't see anything from my perch, but alone in the house, all I cared about was that I couldn't be seen. I waited for another sound, but the soundtrack of the movie drowned out everything else. I counted to thirty and shifted so I could peek through the railing.

The orange-and-white cat slunk through the living room, stopping halfway and looking up at me. He meowed. My eyes had adjusted to the darkness, and from the balcony, I had an opportunity to scan the whole first floor. The cat dashed toward the stairs and ran up them then buzzed my ankles with his fur. I picked him up and scratched his ears.

"Have you been inside this whole time?" I asked him quietly.

He nuzzled my hand and wriggled free of my grasp.

He went down two stairs, turned around, and meowed at me. "I'm coming," I whispered. I followed him down the stairs. He stood up on his hind legs with his paws on the door and scratched. I turned the knob, held it open, and he dashed outside as if he'd just gotten free from a hostage situation. Before I left, I turned back toward the main room and scanned the interior. Something was off, but I couldn't figure out what.

My eyes tracked the room, from the seating area, back to the dining room, and over to the corner where Mysti had set up her booth. That was when I saw—or rather didn't see—the one thing I had expected to see.

The Remington painting over the mantel was missing.

26

THE TOP OF THE LIST OF PEOPLE
WITH MOTIVE

I stared at the empty space on the wall. I was halfway in and halfway out of the house, and I didn't know which was the right way to head.

"Kidd?" Nick asked behind me.

I whirled around and faced him. "The painting's gone." I pointed to the wall.

"Angus took it down earlier today," he said. "Kathy agreed to loan it to a museum in town. They're dropping it off tonight."

"I don't think that's what happened," I said.

I hadn't expected to be gone long enough to arouse suspicion, but just like I understood why Chef might stay with Mysti, I understood why Nick had come to check on me. Now that he was here, I welcomed the opportunity to confide in him.

"Angus found that painting in the trash," I said. "It's an original Remington."

"Lucky for Angus."

"Maybe not," I said. "He's an art historian who specializes in western art. Maybe he didn't just find that painting. It seems like a coincidence, right? He and Joey just happen to be driving through a town on trash day, and he just happens to spot a real Remington propped up against a curb."

"You think Angus arranged to steal it?"

"Maybe. Joey was the only person with him. He could have gotten suspicious. He might have confronted Angus about the painting. Maybe they had a fight, and maybe it didn't turn out so well for Joey."

"You think Angus killed Joey."

"Or maybe," I continued, as if Nick hadn't interjected, "Joey wanted to sell the painting to raise money to pay off the ranch debts. Mysti said it's worth millions. If Joey wanted to sell it, and Angus didn't—"

"Maybe they had a fight, and maybe it didn't turn out so well for Joey," Nick finished.

"So it's not just me, right? You can get there too."

"It's not just you."

"Where did you say Kathy loaned the painting?"

"The Marion Morrison Museum," he said.

"I passed that today. It's not far from the sheriff's station."

"Loncar," we both said at the same time.

I ran to our room and grabbed my phone then called Loncar. I didn't bother with greetings and salutations. "Are you still at the sheriff's office?"

"Not anymore. What happened?" he asked.

"Get the sheriff," I said. "Go to the Marion Morrison Museum. Angus was supposed to deliver a painting for an upcoming exhibit. If it's there, then everything's fine. If not, then Angus is"—I glanced at Nick, and he nodded—"at the top of the list of people with motive for murdering Joey."

"I'll handle it." He disconnected.

I held my phone in my hand, with my knuckles going white around it. "Loncar is going to check out the museum with Sheriff Parker," I said. "What now?"

"Now we go back outside and watch the rest of the movie."

"But—"

"There's nothing you can do about it now."

Doing the responsible thing lacked a certain sense of closure, but I knew Nick was right. Loncar and Parker were on Angus's trail, and soon they'd know if he had done the drop-off at the museum or if he'd skipped town with a multi-million dollar painting in the boot of his car.

As unsatisfied as I was with my role in the evening's unfolding events, a part of me hoped Angus had tried to sneak off with the painting because it meant the rest of us were among friends. If I was wrong, then the murderer was still at large.

A cool breeze swept across my face. It caught the brim of my cowboy hat and blew it off, and the hat tumbled across the dirt road in front of the house and toward the stables. I wouldn't even be wearing the hat if I wasn't trying to fit in. I ran ahead of Nick and chased it across the dirt trail. It felt like a comedy sketch. Each time I closed the distance, the wind kicked back up and carried the hat farther away. A cross breeze caught the brim and sent it into the stables. I ran in and found the hat resting against a bale of hay. I snagged it off the ground and put it on, holding it in place with my hand. I turned around to leave and froze in place when I saw a dirty face staring back at me.

Angus wasn't at the Marion Morrison Museum.

The gray-haired cowboy was in Jupiter's stall, partially hidden by the black gelding. He would have been almost impossible to see if my eyes weren't already adjusted to the darkness. His eyes were what gave him away, white and clear light-blue against the darkness. Behind him, a flat rectangle approximately the size of the missing painting was wrapped in butcher paper and knotted off with twine.

My eyes moved from his face to the package and then back to his face. "You're not supposed to be here," I said. "You're supposed to be delivering that painting to the museum."

"That painting isn't going to the museum," he said.

"But Kathy agreed to loan it to them."

"It's not Kathy's to loan."

"Whose is it? Yours?"

"It's not what you think," he said.

"Then tell me what I should think." I thought about Loncar and Sheriff Parker, who were on their way to the museum to check on Angus's story. I thought about the group of people sitting out front, and the loud sound system that would make it nearly impossible for anyone to hear a call for help.

Angus stepped away from Jupiter, and I backed away.

"I'm not going to hurt you." He held both hands up. "I'm not a killer."

"But you're hiding out in the stables with a stolen painting. Why?"

Angus lowered himself slowly onto a bale of hay. He took his hat off and set it on the ground next to his boots then looked up at me.

"Joey and I got into a fight the other night. That much is true. It was right here, in Jupiter's stall."

"What did you fight about?"

He pointed to the rectangle. "Joey wanted to sell it. He said it would clear the debts on this place and give him a fresh start."

"But the painting wasn't Joey's to sell, was it?"

"We never discussed ownership. I'm the one who spotted it, and I'm the one who knew what it was worth. I always thought of it as mine. It wasn't until that night that I learned Joey thought of it as his."

"What happened?"

"Like I said, we argued. I tried to keep my voice down, but Jupe here got stirred up." He stood up and stroked the horse's mane, keeping his voice steady. "You saved me, didn't you, fella?" He reached into his pocket and pulled out a carrot then held it out while the horse ate it from his outstretched palm.

I stood a few feet away from Angus, watching him feed Jupiter the carrots from his pocket. There was something so gentle about the action that, for the first time since discovering that the famous painting was missing, I doubted Angus was the killer. I didn't run for help, and I didn't try to restrain the cowhand on my own. But while I stood there watching him, another memory pierced my brain. It wasn't Angus. It was the carrot.

Carrots.

A pile of them, sitting out in the kitchen the night the horses got loose, the night I found Joey's body. The very first night we were here. It had seemed odd at the time, but we were guests, and I didn't know the habits of the people here. Carrots were an odd choice of midnight snack, but I'd written it off as the whim of a person who preferred plant-based snacks. It was a testament to my open-mindedness at the time that I hadn't found *that* suspicious.

Jupiter had calmed, thanks to the efforts of Angus. He seemed like a different horse than the agitated one of earlier. He munched on the carrots and made nickering noises to show his appreciation. Angus seemed to have forgotten all about me. He continued speaking in low, even tones. I was close enough to hear the words, all directed to the beautiful black gelding, praising the horse for his majesty. It wasn't a confession of guilt.

Guilty people didn't always rush to admit to their

crimes, but when accused, face-to-face, they often couldn't avoid doing so, especially when they believed, of the two of you, they would be the one walking away. Angus exhibited none of that behavior.

"What happened after the argument?" I wanted to get Angus talking again, to figure out if his affection for Jupiter was just a diversionary tactic.

"I took him out for a ride," he said. "Best way to work off agitation for both horse and rider."

"Is that why you said he saved you? You were angry, and he helped you cool down?"

"Somebody came out here after I left and killed Joey. If I'd still been out here, you might have found my body lying next to his."

"Didn't you need to saddle him up? Wouldn't that take time?"

"Jupiter doesn't mind going bareback when he knows he's got an experienced rider on him." Even though he answered my question, he kept his attention on the horse.

Angus, to anyone watching, was the consummate cowboy. Nothing about him seemed false, phony, or fabricated in order to enhance the atmosphere of the ranch. Even with the knowledge that Angus was one of the region's most respected authenticators of art depicting cowboy life, he looked as if he was exactly where he should be, as if he'd been a part of the Down Home all along.

If I factored in the clues around me, I would have thought Angus was the killer. He'd admitted to an argument with the victim. He'd had both means and motive, and now he was hiding in the stables with a missing painting worth millions of dollars, a painting he claimed belonged to him. But there was something else there, some other piece of information that wanted to burst through my brain, something troubling me.

I thought about what had happened since we arrived. From that very first night, it was one thing after another, starting with Lulu driving into a telephone pole to the horses having gotten out of the stable to Joey being murdered. Then there were Lulu's accident in the arena, the cancellation to the entertainment schedule, and the cut gas line on Tully's truck. I had been relegated to the prima-donna category, left to sleep in every morning while the rest of the group had a dude ranch experience.

It wasn't what I'd wanted, but nobody knew that because I played into their perception of me. I mocked their attire and complained about not having time to read. I watched Nick and Senior jump into the ranch experience, even though their life experiences came from running a shoe company. Even Lulu was more of a trooper than I was. The day after she crashed into a telephone pole, she'd been out on a horse, jumping in the middle of the arena.

A growing sense of unease crept over me. I had an entirely new suspicion, and if I was right, then we'd all been fooled. Loncar was in town with Sheriff Parker, and Nick was outside with the rest of the staff, holding down the fort, waiting for the cavalry to arrive. The problem was we'd all been focused on the wrong motive.

The Remington painting had been on display the entire time. Every employee of the ranch knew how it came to be hanging above the mantel. Mysti told me the story, her pride in Angus evident. The story underscored the caliber of the staff at the Down Home. I could say some negative things about the employees, but they took pride in their work. Angus, Cody, Chef, Tully—they all wanted what was best for the Down Home.

Pieces of information that I hadn't considered part of the same data set came together and created a new picture, and I started to see what had eluded me all along.

27

WHY DENY IT?

I REACHED INTO MY POCKET AND PULLED OUT THE GOLD nail that I'd found inside the arena. The flyer that had been left on Kathy's SUV at the Boot Strap fell to the floor. I bent down, picked it up, and looked at Angus.

"Have you seen this before?" I asked Angus.

"Sure," he said. "Trick riders put them on the windshields in town a couple days before their events."

"I meant the nail."

He shrugged. "Horseshoe nails are a dime a dozen around these parts. Joey had a couple dozen of them dipped in gold to sell as keepsakes, but they never took off."

"I found it in the arena after Lulu's accident. Do you know how it could have gotten there?"

He shook his head. "Joey carried one around with him, sort of a good-luck charm, but I can't see how it got from his pocket to the arena, not with his body being in here."

Ever since I had arrived, I slotted people into roles based on how they presented themselves. At first, I saw them as clichés, characters from movies, TV shows, and pop culture that painted a picture of ranch life. It had taken me a few days on the ranch to understand that those characters existed in pop culture because they existed in real life. It was art imitating life, not the other way around.

But the more I thought about it, the more I saw that one person *wasn't* what she seemed. From her arrival, she'd literally crashed the place and made us all think she was more out of place than I was.

But an inexperienced visitor to a dude ranch wouldn't mount a horse and try to jump in front of a crowd of ranch hands and spectators. I knew that because that was exactly what I was—an inexperienced visitor to a dude ranch. All along, I'd been exactly what I was.

I jammed the nail back into my pocket and unfolded the flyer for the trick rodeo. The page was overcrowded with information about jumpers and stunt performers and even listed the Yee Haws as the headlining musical act for tomorrow night—the real reason they'd canceled on the Down Home. I scanned the images and the captions, and on the bottom right of the page, I saw a grainy photo of two rodeo clowns. The image was unclear, thanks to a copier malfunction, but under the makeup, one of the faces was familiar. It confirmed my mounting suspicions. It was Lulu.

A visitor to a dude ranch wouldn't know how to take a fall from a horse, but a rodeo clown would.

"It's Lulu," I said to Angus. I held the flyer toward him, and he took it. But before he had a chance to figure out why I had drawn that conclusion, something small hit my butt cheek. I jumped and turned around. A tranquilizer dart, identifiable by the fluffy pink carnation-like protrusion on one end, lay on the ground next to my boot. I felt over my ass where it had hit me, and my fingers landed on the thick leather Wrangler patch on Loncar's jeans. One inch lower, and I would be face down on the hay.

Lulu Cassidy stood just inside the stables. A tranquilizer gun dangled from her hand. "Talking to the horses?" she asked. "Too bad they don't know how to call the cops."

"I was talking to—" I turned around and looked for Angus. He wasn't there. I had no idea where he could have gone, but for the moment, it seemed wiser to let Lulu think she was facing down one of us and to keep Angus's presence to myself. "Jupiter," I finished.

"Right," she said. "If that horse didn't help Joey, I doubt he'll help you."

"Then you don't deny you were the one to murder Joey?"

"Why deny it? I just shot you with a tranq. No point playing coy now."

My eyes glanced to the floor. The dart intended to incapacitate me lay next to the toe of my cowboy boot. Lulu was about ten feet away. Even if I bent down to grab the dart and charged her, I would accomplish little more than improving her odds of hitting me the next time.

"Why use a tranquilizer gun?" I asked. "I'll just wake up and tell everybody you're the murderer."

"That implies they'll find you," she said, "and you're a loose end I don't plan to leave behind."

I gulped. It was dark, and we were surrounded by crowded tree lines and empty acreage for twenty miles. The soundtrack from the movie would have drowned out any noises coming from the stables. Nick was the only one besides Angus who knew where I was, and the fact that he hadn't come looking for me meant something more pressing must have happened. "Where's Nick?"

"With his dad."

"What did you do to him?"

"He'll be fine," she said. "They'll all be fine once they recover from the horse tranquilizers I ground up and mixed into the popcorn seasoning." She laughed. "It's easy to taint the food source when you're the sole vegan in the group."

"Senior is a seventy-five-year-old man," I said. "He didn't do anything to you."

"He wants to buy the place. Nobody should want to invest in this property after what we did. Accidents, arguments, infighting. Joey had this place leveraged up to his eyeballs. He had one choice—sell it to me."

"For what?"

"To chop up and sell off for profit. There's no future for a place like this. It takes dedication to run a cattle ranch, and it takes a talented breeder to produce a stable of horses that can turn a profit. Tully's an old man. Angus is too. Kathy keeps Cody around because she's sleeping with him, and Chef's going to be out of a job as soon as word about the food poisoning gets out. The Down Home is imploding as we speak." She glanced at her watch. "Right on schedule."

"But this place has been here for generations," I said. "You can't just destroy that."

"Why not? Nobody else here cares enough to keep it going. You and your family don't know the first thing about horses. I found that out the night I arrived. When I first heard I was going to be here with another interested party, I worried that you might make things difficult for me, so I beat you to the punch. There's nothing like a car accident and an overbearing spouse to cast a wife as the victim."

"You drove your car into a phone pole," I said. "Nobody's crazy enough to risk their lives for a little misdirection."

"Oh, please," she said. "I'm a rodeo clown. I make my living by sitting in a barrel while an angry bull charges me. Do you think a fender bender was going to stop me?"

"But I saw it happen. It wasn't a fender bender."

"It was. It just didn't happen that night. And if I recall,

you fell in the mud on your way to rescue me. You didn't have time to *see* anything."

I hated that she was right. I'd been on the porch with Nick, staring out at the clear sky. It was shortly after we arrived, and I wanted to sit outside and breathe in the cool, crisp night air. When Lulu and Billy drove down the dirt road, I was in mid-protestation mode, still thinking of this whole thing as being a joke—*not* a legitimate business venture, or a worthwhile way to decompress, or a new experience that could broaden my mind. I was distracted from reality, so much so that I didn't even question how there'd been no rain to saturate the ground. The accident had kept me from getting past my self-imposed short-sightedness, giving me an excuse to be the person I always was—someone who charged into situations trying to help, not seeing things clearly.

Whether it was because of the week on the ranch or Lulu's cool calmness, tonight, I viewed things differently.

"You were the one in the kitchen last night," I said. "You heard me talking to Loncar. You know—" I stopped speaking abruptly.

So much of what I'd taken for granted appeared to be fake, and I hadn't seen it. Joey and Kathy weren't a happily married couple looking to sell off the ranch so they could enjoy the next chapter of their lives. They had been on the brink of divorce and eager to get away from each other. Angus wasn't a bitter cowboy; he was a former art historian. Henna wasn't just a laundromat employee;

she was an award-winning barrel racer. Mysti wasn't just a flighty spiritual guide; she was a trained psychologist.

And Lulu. She wasn't just a visitor to the ranch; she was an opportunistic land baron who didn't care about the people who had made the Down Home the Down Home. She didn't care about anything but herself.

Which didn't bode particularly well for me.

Except I wasn't the only person who'd made snap judgments about the group. Lulu had too. She would have been able to research Kathy, Joey, Angus, Cody, Henna, and Mysti, but she couldn't know anything about me, Nick, Senior, or Loncar. She couldn't know anything we hadn't allowed her to.

I closed my eyes briefly and reviewed my actions since we had arrived. If somebody didn't know me, what conclusions would they have reached about me?

I hadn't spent time with Nick—not on early morning rides or trips into town. I argued with his dad and ate by myself. I invited another man to the ranch and spent more time with him than with my husband. I was even wearing his pants.

"You know I'm sleeping with Loncar," I said, finishing my sentence. "I thought we were doing a good job of hiding it, but I guess not." I forced a chuckle. "You probably noticed the wear marks on my jeans are the same as his. We arranged to meet out here while everybody else was out front watching the movie."

"Charlie Loncar went into town with Sheriff Parker."

"No, he didn't," I said. "When you're stepping out on your husband, it's good to have a cover story."

For the first time since Lulu entered the stables, she looked lost. She turned her head toward the entrance.

The seed of doubt was all I needed. I scanned my surroundings and grabbed the closest thing to me—a coil of rope. It was heavier than I expected, and I stumbled under its weight. Lulu turned back to face me. I threw the whole coil at her and dropped to the ground. I grabbed the loose tranquilizer dart. I crawled into Jupiter's stall and pressed myself against the barrier, digging the heels of my boots into the packed dirt floor for purchase while clutching the dart and listening to the sounds of her approach.

But Jupiter, the beautiful black gelding, was spooked by my sudden appearance in his stall. He stomped his feet and whinnied. I heard a sharp *crack!* Jupe reared up on his hind legs and charged out of his stall. In a blur, Angus raced out behind him.

A scream.

A thud.

A gunshot.

I didn't have to see Lulu to know the raging black gelding had taken her by surprise, but my heart clenched as I imagined who had been on the receiving end of that gunshot.

"You can come out now," said a male voice. "We got her."

I stood on shaky legs and put my hands on the bale of

hay to steady myself. I came out from the stable. Angus was standing over Lulu. Her head hung listlessly to the side. A trail of drool trickled from between her lips and dripped onto her bedazzled cowgirl shirt. Her arms were bound to her sides with rope, like a calf that had been lassoed during a contest. Angus stood behind her, and Tully stood next to Angus. Lulu's tranquilizer gun was in Tully's hand.

"Not bad, Ms. Kidd," Tully said. "Maybe we'll make a cowgirl out of you yet."

28

THE STUFF OF NIGHTMARES

LET'S BE HONEST. THERE WAS NO WAY THE COIL OF ROPE I'D thrown at Lulu had conveniently landed around her arms, restraining her from shooting at me or Jupiter, but no matter how many times the rest of the group pressed Tully and Angus, that was the story they told. By the time we went home, it would be the stuff of legend.

While I was in the stable, a few other things were going down. Loncar was in town with Sheriff Parker, just like I'd thought, but while they shared notes, it wasn't the Remington painting they discussed. It was the identity of a rodeo clown who'd been spotted on a nearby surveillance camera the same day the gas line of Tully's truck had been cut. Clown makeup might be enough to keep a person from being picked out of a lineup, but facial recognition software saw past the makeup and provided a hit. The clown was Billy Cassidy.

Once Sheriff Parker and Loncar figured out Billy's

identity, it was a short step—or rather, a half block—to the Boot Strap, where they found Maverick, the town's so-called social director, who gave them a copy of the flyer that promoted the trick rodeo. Maverick had no reason to be suspicious of the rodeo clown who had entered the Boot Strap, but his bar had been the convergence point for the rest of the clues Parker had amassed.

Such as Angus's truck. My theory about someone sawing through the gas line wasn't far off. Both Billy and Lulu had been in town that day, one disguised as a rodeo clown to hijack attention while the other cut through the gas line. They didn't use a hockey stick, but they had used a knife. The garage where the truck had been towed confirmed that to Sheriff Parker, who didn't have the courtesy to let me know I was half right until well after the fact.

Men.

Two plus two equaled four, and Parker issued a warrant for Lulu and Billy's arrests. The whole thing might have ended there if Billy hadn't slipped pulverized horse tranquilizers into the kettle corn prior to movie night, making the Down Home look like a sightly disturbing sleepover. That was the scene Tully and I discovered after we left Lulu tied to the hitching post. Tully straddled Strawberry and went after Jupiter, my real savior, the wild card that had probably done more to incapacitate Lulu than anything I could have attempted. Jupe was due for a lifetime supply of sugar cubes and carrots, if I had anything to say about it.

Finding your loved ones and vacation family in a dosed stupor while a distorted projection of *Red River* splashed against an exterior wall was the stuff of nightmares. One by one, Tully and I rousted each person long enough for a member of a medical unit to give them the once-over and declare that they'd be fine once they slept off the drugs. It was a clear night, under a starry sky, and it was far easier to bring pillows outside than to move everyone inside. Angus provided sleeping bags, blankets, and pillows, and before long, we had ourselves an outdoor campsite.

————

IT TOOK forty-eight hours before the full effects of the drugs left everyone's systems and seventy-two before the atmosphere of the ranch turned joyful again. While Nick, his dad, Mysti, Chef, Kathy, and Cody slept off the side effects, I got a crash course in ranch life. Each morning I dressed in a faded chambray shirt and a pair of Loncar's jeans. Tully borrowed a gentle colt named Susie from the nearby Tomlin farm and taught me the basics of riding. I stood in for Chef and collected eggs in the morning and went out with Tully and Loncar to exercise horses as the sun rose and again as it fell. I discovered muscles I didn't know my body had. Each day, I wore a fresh bandana, and by the third day, my new boots were close to having been broken in.

Inevitably, word about the trouble at the Down Home

spread through town. By the time Chef was able to assume his regular role, I'd introduced a steady stream of sympathetic and interested parties to hot-dog shish kebobs, cornbread casserole, and wagon wheel mac and cheese. Chef even found a clone recipe of Butterscotch Krimpets to make at the suggestion of Loncar.

The one thing nobody wanted was popcorn.

————

FOUR DAYS after my showdown with Lulu. Chef, finally fully recovered, defrosted steaks and fired up the grill. The extent of my assistance was wrapping potatoes in tinfoil. After that, I was sent out front to join the rest of the group. Two tall stools were propped on the carpet in front of the fire, where a group of men I hadn't met had gathered. A bass drum nearby contained the name Yee Haws, and one of the musicians had a pair of drumsticks sticking out of his back pocket. I was disappointed that Loncar wouldn't be taking the stage in his role as lead singer of Backup, but in the bigger picture, I was happy we'd all survived.

Nick slung his arm around me. "You did it again, Kidd," he said then pressed his lips against my temple.

"Barely."

I looked around the room. Maverick had joined us, and he stood next to Loncar, with a guitar in his hands. On the other side of the room, Mysti braided Henna's hair. The Remington painting had been returned to the wall over the mantel, and this time, with the benefit of the knowledge I'd gained from a week here, I appreciated the depiction of the cowboy. I couldn't believe how easily I'd dismissed it when we first arrived a week ago. My eyes had been opened to so much more than a western dude ranch experience, and I knew I would never be the same.

Angus, Senior, and Tully were a few feet away, drinking beer. Kathy and Cody were seated at the table, deep in conversation.

"Wait here, would you?" I asked.

"Sure," he said.

I left Nick and approached the group of men. "There she is," Senior said. He raised his beer bottle in my direction, and Angus and Tully followed suit. I was embarrassed by the attention. "The one who saved the day," Senior added.

"I got lucky," I said.

"That's not what Tully tells me." Senior looked at Tully, who kept his eyes on me.

Of everybody here, Tully was the only person who knew what had gone down in the stables. He spotted Lulu moments before she fired the tranquilizer dart at me and hid behind Jupiter to formulate a plan. After I distracted her with the coil of rope, Tully slapped Jupiter's haunches to send him thundering out of his stall.

I didn't think Jupiter had been the one to shoot Lulu with a tranquilizer dart, but that would be one mystery that nobody bothered to solve.

"So," I said to Senior, "are you still thinking of buying the place?"

"Can't," Senior said. "I got outbid." He tapped the neck of his beer bottle against Tully's and left me to join Nick across the room.

I was nervous to be alone with Tully, not because he scared me—I knew the threat was gone the moment Lulu and Billy were carted off with Sheriff Parker—but because he knew things about me that might have led him to draw the wrong conclusions.

"I still can't figure out why Angus acted so suspiciously," I said.

"A lot of evidence pointed at him," Tully said. "When I found the painting in Jupiter's stall, I admit I suspected him myself. We all know how valuable it is, but he's the only one here who would know what to do with it." He took a pull on his beer. "You know what I can't figure out?" He stared across the room in the same direction I did, but I didn't think he was talking about anyone present.

"What?"

"Why you avoided us all week." He turned to face me, and I studied him. His red hair was a vibrant contrast to the bisque-colored walls behind him, and his blue eyes popped against his tan and freckled face. His chambray shirt was unbuttoned a few buttons, and a tuft of chest hair peeked out.

"I never felt welcome," I said. "From the moment we arrived, Angus and Cody acted like I was in the way. After

I found Joey's body, you treated me like I was the one who let out the horses. Until Mysti showed up, the person who seemed the most like me was Lulu, but even she acted as if she'd been looking forward to this trip for months. She looked like she bought out a Boot Barn for this week. That's something I would do."

"Why didn't you?"

"It felt like a costume. Like I would have been trying to be someone I wasn't."

"You borrowed clothes from your detective friend. Isn't that a form of costume?" Tully asked.

I sighed. "There have been times in my life when clothes were like armor. Like I could do anything, if I dressed the part. I thought if I looked like I fit in, the week might be less painful."

"You never looked like you fit in." At my surprised expression, he added, "I never thought you were cheating on your husband, but I noticed your jeans the moment you walked in. You looked too much the part to be as out of place as you were. Your actions didn't match your appearance. From the moment I met you, I thought you were hiding something."

"Trust me, I'm exactly what I seem."

"You're about as far from what you seem as a person could be, but the only person here who got to see that was me. As long as you're still on the ranch, maybe you should do something about that."

It sounded like an invitation.

Before I had a chance to respond, Kathy stood and

clinked her spoon against her coffee cup. Slowly, conversations around us faded until the room was silent and she was the center of attention.

"It's been a crazy week around here. A lot has happened, and the Down Home is never going to be the same."

If the room hadn't already gone silent, the reality of what Kathy was saying would have quieted it. We all stood around, waiting to hear what she wanted to announce.

"There's been a lot of gossip about what's to become of the ranch," she continued. "I'd like to put that gossip to rest and introduce the new owner of the Down Home."

She turned to Cody, who stood. He removed his cowboy hat and held it over his heart. "I've been waiting for the tides to turn my way for a long time. I promise the Down Home will continue to be what y'all want it to be—hospitality, horses, and heart."

A round of supportive applause and a few hoots and hollers went up around the room.

I leaned toward Angus. "So they're not sleeping together?"

"Oh, they're sleeping together," Angus said with a wink. "Sometimes things are *exactly* what they seem."

DESIGNER DIRTY LAUNDRY
KILLER FASHION MYSTERY #1

In case you missed how it all began (or want to see how far Samantha Kidd has come!)

DESIGNER DIRTY LAUNDRY
CHAPTER 1: IT ALL STARTED TO GO WRONG

When you wear fishnet stockings to the grocery store, people tend to stare. Women look at you like you're affiliated with the sex trade. Men pretend they're not staring, doing so all the while. It's probably because they're thinking the same thing.

The last time I wore fishnets to the grocery store was weeks ago. It was then I met the man who changed the course of my life. Because of him, I'd traded in the title of senior buyer of ladies designer shoes at Bentley's New York to become the trend specialist at Tradava, the family-owned retailer in Ribbon, Pennsylvania. I'd given up an apartment in Manhattan to buy the house where I grew up. And now, because of him, I sat in a police station explaining my actions to a homicide detective.

I still couldn't pinpoint exactly when it all started to go wrong.

A week earlier . . .

I changed clothes six times, then ultimately settled on the fashion uniform of black: satin motorcycle jacket cinched at the waist over a lace camisole, pegged pencil skirt, fishnets, and stilettos. Elsa Klensch meets Catwoman. Patrick, the fashion director and my new boss, was bound to approve. I topped off my look with a finishing blast of Aqua Net, powered up with coffee and a donut from a newspaper kiosk by my house, and headed to work earlier than I remember ever going to work before.

I arrived at Tradava and followed a trickle of other early employees into the building. A petite Latina woman in an oversized pink sweater and black leggings struggled to carry a box through the door marked "Loss Prevention."

"Let me help you," I called out. I raced forward with my arms out. The woman pivoted, and I grabbed ahold of the other side of the box just as she was about to lose control. She inched her way backward and together, we got it through the door.

"Set it on the floor," she said. We both bent down, her in the manner the How to Lift Properly posters advised and me in a way that would surely make my back stiff in an hour. The box thumped onto the exposed concrete floor. The woman straightened up and smiled. "Thanks," she said. "That box just about killed me." She

studied my face. "Are you a vendor? Let me get the sign-in log."

"I'm Samantha Kidd," I said. "Patrick's new trend specialist. Do you know if he's here yet?"

"He's here, but he didn't say anything about you." Her brow furrowed, and she picked up the phone and dialed an extension. When no one answered, she hung up.

"He's not in the office. You'll have to sign in like a visitor."

"But I'm not a visitor. I'm staff. Today's my first day."

The friendly vibe we'd had after I helped her with the box that almost killed her had waned, but she *did* seem conflicted. "Do you have ID?" she asked hopefully.

I reached into my handbag and pulled out a quilted leather wallet, then held it open to show my driver's license through the plastic window.

"I meant a store ID."

"No. Not yet, anyway."

"That's a New York license," she commented.

"You're right, I just moved. But it's me, see?" I held the wallet up to my face and smiled at her in the way only a half crazy person brimming with caffeine and adrenaline over starting a new job might.

The woman reached her hands up and gathered her long, wavy, brownish-orange hair on top of her head then wound it around several times until it resembled a doorknob. She pushed the sign-in log toward me and held out a red ballpoint pen. "I'm sure you'll get it all straightened out today."

"Right," I said. Look at me, already making friends! I signed my name with a flourish then added *Trend office, 7:37.* I put my wallet back in my handbag, then hopped out of the way of a flatbed filled with merchandise and headed into the store. Aside from security and shipping, the store was quiet.

I wasn't a morning person. It was day one of a new job and a new life. Full of potential. My early arrival had less to do with my natural inclinations and more to do with my need to make a good impression. I was determined to be the best trend specialist Patrick had ever hired.

I wandered through the shoe department on my way to the elevators, pausing by a round marble fixture that displayed a purple suede platform pump. My index finger traced over the black and white designer label that decorated the sock lining.

"Of all the shoes, in all the stores, she had to walk up to mine," said a husky voice behind me. I turned and faced the man whose name was stitched onto that label. The man I'd once fantasized about during a layover in Paris. The man I'd almost kissed after a business dinner that involved a good deal of Sauvignon Blanc and a serving of lemon meringue pie. My judgment is not to be trusted around lemon meringue.

Nick Taylor was a shoe designer. His showroom was charged with electricity, hot looks, and devastating style. His shoe collection wasn't bad, either. He was one of the few people I thought I'd miss after leaving Bentley's, that is, until I caught him flirting with the buyer from

Bloomingdales and realized the only special thing we had was a gross margin agreement.

"You're a long way from New York," I said. "What are you doing at Tradava?"

"Same thing as you, probably."

"I doubt that. I'm here to start a new job." I cocked my head to the side and crossed my arms, the plum-colored laptop bag that hung from my shoulder now banging against my hip.

"First day? Let's get you into practice." He stood directly in front of me and held out his hand. "I'm Nick Taylor. Shoe designer and all around good guy."

I pursed my lips and took in his dark curly hair and his brown eyes, the exact shade of the three root beer barrels I ate in the car after finishing the donut. I met his outstretched hand with my own.

"Samantha Kidd. Former shoe buyer. Former angry New Yorker." I pumped his hand twice to emphasize the word 'former.' "Current trend specialist for Tradava on the cusp of a new life."

He pulled me in, converting our handshake to an embrace. I lost my balance and fell against him. "I thought I might never see you again," he whispered in my ear. "So, Tradava?" He looked to his left and right as if making sure no one was listening. "From the big city to the small town. I knew you'd land on your feet, but I didn't expect you to land here."

"You make it sound like I vanished into the night," I replied, blowing at a strand of hair that had gotten stuck in my lipstick. My cell phone buzzed from the depths of my handbag, and I pretended not to hear it.

"You did vanish in the night. Out of my life, out of my dreams . . . " He reached out an index finger and freed the lock of hair. A trace of red lipstick transferred to his fingertip. "And now I find you haven't even missed me. That hurts."

"So you took it upon yourself to stalk me. Good to know."

"C'mon, everybody needs at least one stalker in their life. It's good for the ego," he said.

Nick Taylor had captured the eye of more than one female at Bentley's, and rumors of his love life often permeated the otherwise work-heavy market weeks. More than once I'd wondered what would have happened if I'd given in to my post-pie impulse to kiss him after that innocent business dinner last May.

"You didn't answer my question. What are you doing at Tradava this early?"

"I have some outstanding business with the shoe buyer," he said. "The only time he had available was this morning."

"Did security make you sign in?" I asked, nodding toward the back hallway.

"Sure. They make everybody sign in before the store is open."

The elevator bell sounded. The doors attempted to open, then jerked shut. Nick stabbed the button with his index finger, and the doors repeated their spastic motion.

I had the other option to take the stairs but with a breakfast of highly concentrated sugar, fat, and root beer barrels coursing through my veins, that wasn't going to happen.

The doors jerked open again, and I jammed the laptop between them. They beat an irregular rhythm against the plum nylon case but left a resulting opening large enough for my fingers. By now I had exerted more energy than I would have on the stairs, but I was determined to get on the thing.

I quickly changed my mind.

In the elevator was a well-dressed man. His jet-black hair was held perfectly in place with pomade, and his mustache was neatly trimmed. He wore a taupe suit with a violet windowpane pattern, a brown and purple paisley ascot knotted around his neck, and a crisp white shirt that no doubt had been laundered and starched by a team of professionals. Even though his body lay crumpled on the floor, the shirt was barely wrinkled.

Patrick.

My new boss.

I yanked the laptop out from between the doors. When I stood back up, the room spun. I put a hand out to steady myself and lost my grip on the computer bag. It fell from my shoulder and landed on its side.

My knees buckled, and I followed the laptop to the floor.

ABOUT THE AUTHOR

National bestselling author Diane Vallere writes smart, funny, and fashionable character-based mysteries. After two decades working for a top luxury retailer, she traded fashion accessories for accessories to murder. A past president of Sisters in Crime, Diane started her own detective agency at age ten and has maintained a passion for shoes, clues, and clothes ever since. Find out more at dianevallere.com.

ACKNOWLEDGMENTS

Thank you for reading Samantha Kidd's latest mystery. Ever since she made a disparaging comment about western attire back in her first mystery, I knew someday we'd come face to face with that trend. It took a binge of first Yellowstone, and then Longmire to nudge me (and her) into action.

Astute readers will recognize the horses names (Starlight, Jupiter, and Susie) as coming straight from the pages of Trixie Belden books. Trixie was my first mystery love, so I couldn't not take a moment to pay a small tribute to that series.

Thank you to Red Adept Editing for notes on this manuscript, and to Panera for giving me a writing office away from home. Thank you to the Polyester Posse, for helping to spread the word about this book, to my writing group for helping me work out the story kinks as they appeared, and to my inner circle of friends and family who help me remember there is life outside of a working manuscript.

Most of all, thank you to you, dear reader, for buying my books and reading my stories. This marks number forty, which never would have happened without you.

ALSO BY

<u>Samantha Kidd Mysteries</u>

Designer Dirty Laundry

Buyer, Beware

The Brim Reaper

Some Like It Haute

Grand Theft Retro

Pearls Gone Wild

Cement Stilettos

Panty Raid

Union Jacked

Slay Ride

Tough Luxe

Fahrenheit 501

Stark Raving Mod

Gilt Trip

Ranch Dressing

<u>Madison Night Mad for Mod Mysteries</u>

"Midnight Ice" (prequel novella)

Pillow StalkThat Touch of Ink

With Vics You Get Eggroll

The Decorator Who Knew Too Much

The Pajama Frame

Lover Come Hack

Apprehend Me No Flowers

Teacher's Threat

The Kill of It All

Love Me or Grieve Me

Please Don't Push Up the Daisies

The Glass Bottom Hoax

<u>Sylvia Stryker Outer Space Mysteries</u>

Murder on a Moon Trek

Scandal on a Moon Trek

Hijacked on a Moon Trek

Framed on a Moon Trek

Warped on a Moon Trek

<u>Material Witness Mysteries</u>

Suede to Rest

Crushed Velvet

Silk Stalkings

Tulle Death Do Us Part

<u>Costume Shop Mystery Series</u>

A Disguise to Die For

Masking for Trouble

Dressed to Confess

<u>Mermaid Mysteries</u>

Dead in the Water

<u>Non-Fiction</u>

Bonbons for your Brain